# Tyro's Journey

**Tyro's Journey**
is the third book in the Burnchester mystery,
which was begun with
**The Mysterious Burnchester Hall**
and continued in
**The Burnchester Dome and the Sacred Cell**

# Tyro's Journey

Dominic Miéville

DM
Productions

Published by
DM
PRODUCTIONS
PO Box 218 IP22 1QY United Kingdom

Copyright © 2009 Dominic Miéville

First impression June 2009

The right of Dominic Miéville to be recognised as the author
of this work has been asserted in accordance with
the Copyright, Designs and Patents Act 1988

British Library Cataloguing in Publication Data
A Catalogue record of this book is available from
The British Library

ISBN 978 0 953 6161 6 9

Cover design by Luke Florio

Typesetting by Rowland Phototypesetting Ltd
Bury St Edmunds, Suffolk IP32 6NU
Set in Palatino and Centaur

Printed in Great Britain by
TJ International Ltd
Padstow, Cornwall PL28 8RW

For my father
and in memory of CCM

not forgetting
Rosie

# I

THE OLD HALL, HAYDON. SOME YEARS LATER

"I will try my best to tell it as it happened, but there is never an exact beginning, just a moment, or moments, that seem to lead to change. Where does a journey begin exactly, and does it ever really end? In some ways I wish it hadn't started, but I must not complain about that now. It is no good trying to deny what is written."

I put the book down, and look at my child in her bed. My diary seemed to talk to her as if they were twins. But she is asleep now, and the book closed.

Before leaving the room, I look out of the window. The window onto my early world, the canvas of my adventures, from which I could create the future. Like the window of my dreams, opening onto the past and leading me on. This compulsion has always been my fate, energy and insight, my mother called it. I do not know. I have been on many journeys and have learned less than I had hoped, except that the wheel does not cease from spinning.

"I want to know what happened, Mummy, after the fire, when...."

My little girl had seemed to pause, as if, she being me, could tell what might happen and didn't want to spoil it for herself.

"Later, darling. You must sleep now," I had said. "By the

time you wake up, Daddy will be back to take you to school. That will be nice, won't it?"

I wish.... but no! Enough of that. I am older now.

I descend the stairs and enter the garden. The night air helps to filter time so that the past and the present are one.

My own story returns to me, like a forgotten guest.

By the pond at the front of the house, the splash of fish breaks the water. Our cat Biscuit (who will live forever) watches from the bushes, swishing his old tail from side to side. I look over the lawn, then at the trees at the edge of the drive, where I went alone that night, with Rompy.

I can just make out the outline of the Church of All Saints, beyond. The old yew, beneath which Rick descended into the tunnel, stands secure. The ancient standing stone keeps watch over the graves. In front of it is a chimney-like flue, with a flat top. Around this are twelve crystal shapes pointing upwards. They rotate very slowly about a central metal wire, each giving off a different light.

Dennis' trip mirrors are no longer active. There are no shadows now, only the natural shades of night. On the tower, where climbing irons were once embedded, nothing remains.

Close to the chimney is a young tree. It is fenced in for now, until the fruit ripen.

I look up at the night sky.

Somewhere above us is the constellation.

I look at my daughter's window and imagine her looking out. Her own dreams will take her there.

Would she see me against the trees? How will I take part in her memory; the past and future standing side by side, carrying her forward?

The passing clouds filter the full moon.

A bat crosses the night.

I will try to meet my daughter in her dreams.

2

I enter the house and sit at my desk. On it stands a beautiful medallion.

I pick my special writing pen, and begin....

*

OUTER LONDON, PRESENT. DAYS AFTER THE SEA JOURNEY

.... I am exhausted from nights of flight and have reached the city at last.

I hope that nobody suspects that I have survived.

I am barely able to carry my few belongings, a few papers and the cell.

Reports say that Burnchester Hall remains surrounded and sealed. Nobody has been able to enter or leave. Except for the figures who followed us.

I have heard nothing of Shingle Island. Nor of my friends, Jess and Rick. I hope they are alive.

The horror of that night comes back to me. The slaughter of the soldiers. The escape by boat, the final terror, and my return ashore, from which I have journeyed here.

Jess and Rick's faces come at me like unsaid prayers, reminding me of their capture and their love.

I walk beside graffitied walls, close to warehouses by the river.

I reach a crowded street, lower my eyes, turn away, ignore voices.

I wish I could be anywhere but this dread place, where only the sky connects me with my first world. Yet around me people's hearts beat. It is less easy to be brave alone.

A mother is with her child. Two lovers walk along, arm in arm. A group of players perform street theatre.

A gradual smile crosses my face. I think of Mr Baxter. I was one of the witches once. Next time I shall play Lady Macbeth, if Shakespeare will have me.

Is this the journey that Mr Rummage envisaged? I have let him down.

I want to fly again. I want to tell the world my secret – albeit it is history now – of the cell that I carry. But I cannot, for I do not know its meaning. And I have been sworn to silence.

I want to return to my old life, but the past plays tricks by its deceit and will not free me until the time is right, and of course, I hate to say it, when it is transformed, "Deo concedente", "according to the will of God". How I hate that phrase.

Yes, I know. I know it reader. Please do not remind me. I, like you, have been sworn to secrecy. In that we share an unlocked heart. I carry something – I can only say this from what I have been told – from which a future spark will spring, that will bring light. Many people want its power.

I must be careful who I befriend.

I was given it by Tom, in the presence of the serpent who lies at the base of all things, and dreams of eternal power, as King of this Earth. He who enters into the souls of those who seek power alone.

I will not relinquish the cell until it has led me to its home.

Everywhere the virus spreads, according to Mr Rummage, over the dark land. Creeping greed and corruption. Disillusion, all over the world. The "ceremony of innocence", drowned.

I recall the white-robed figure in the Burnchester Dome. I do not know what the apparition was. An image from the painting brought out by a curious conjunction of energies in time and place. In the realm between my own imagination and the borderland between it and the world. An image whose time has passed. One that passed its gift via Tom to me. To us all.

I feel older than I am. I sense the mantle of my mother on me, and the spirit of my father too, though he is gone. I would do anything to find him again. To hear him call my name.

I reach a bridge that crosses a railway line. I stumble against the bridge wall and strike my head. I try to be sick.

When I look up, I see a man watching me from across the road. He turns his back, as if to speak to someone. The shadow of a cross reflects across his back. They have found me again.

I hurry forward, wiping the cut on my forehead, and turn. The figure has gone.

Over the bridge there are shops and people. Someone offers to help but I wave her away.

Outside a newsagent the evening headlines read:

"Army assault imminent at captured school. Mystery deepens."

"Government in crisis over Shingle Island. Calls for PM to resign."

"Police lose control. Vigilantes roam unchecked."

I look at the first article. The reporter's name is Andrew Veech, Mr Rummage's friend. Has he escaped from the Dome? If not, how is he getting his reports out?

I take a paper from the stand. I must find him.

\*

Not far above Tyro, a helicopter scours the sky, moving towards the City's towers.

The pilot watches for the landing pad below. Mr Vespers is well trained.

"You are certain?"

The man who has just spoken is large and dressed in a suit. He carries a briefcase. We have seen him before in another place, though he inhabits many; sometimes, it seems, simultaneously.

"Certain."

The man breathes, almost with a smile, into the speaker.

"There must be no mistake. She must lead us to.... and then...."

"No mistake."

A third man sits behind the pilot. His hands are tied. Beside him another pair of hands, belonging to Mr Blakemore, hold a gun to the prisoner's head.

The large man scans the horizon, then looks down. He is impatient, but he has made a pact. He will have the cell, whatever the cost.

His power grows across the globe. The will to power is greater than the will to live, except that for him they are indistinguishable.

By then he will own time.

*

I sit outside a cafe, warily, and begin to read.

"The situation at Burnchester Hall remains critical. For days there has been no sign of our good people, no sign of the figures, no activity at all under the Dome, though the school, we can see from the charred remains of one of the buildings, has been badly damaged by fire. There is no information about casualties. Every effort to enter has failed. Every effort to make contact has come to nothing. We can only fear the worst.

The Ministry of Defence refuses to comment on any aspect of the situation, not least the efforts by our Special Forces to enter the tunnels, whose existence they still deny. I have seen some of them myself.

As for the secret research station beneath the site, it is feared that it has been taken over.

Its work – we can exclusively reveal – is "above top secret". Rumour suggests research into deep space penetration. My colleagues and I have tried to discover more, but we meet a wall of silence. It seems that only a very few know of the project.

When our forces attack, which seems imminent, the danger

to staff, parents and children will be considerable. If they delay, the occupants might not survive.

Having been sworn to secrecy by Mr Rummage – a key player in this mystery – I know that force would be a serious mistake. I have been present at many of the events that have occurred. Some are bewildering, most inexplicable, all fraught with danger.

I am trying to piece together fragments of the story. We are searching all avenues, exploring possibilities, unearthing contacts close to the ground, to see if there are any clues to unravelling the mystery.

The whereabouts of Mr Gatherin, the veteran of the former World War Two spy school, and his colleague M. Le Petit, are not known. Why were the Burnchester Arms men not responding to the emergency calls from inside and outside the school? It is believed that they were not trapped in the Dome with the others. Where are they?

Nobody is quite sure who is to blame, but chief suspects are the Priory, whose agents have been seen in the vicinity for some time.

One thing we do know. Behind those who are responsible is one known as the Stranger, and behind him an overwhelming force of darkness, incarnated in a shadowy figure called the Dark Master. It is believed that his energy and capabilities act like a virus, spreading through those who can be corrupted or bribed, led by the King of the world, known as the Other. The King who would rule the world for his own ends.

The whereabouts of Tyro and her friends, who are thought to have escaped, is not known. It is perhaps better that way. It may be their only chance. If they are caught, we are all lost.

My location is secret. This report may have been vetted.

Anyone with information should contact the number below. If Tyro reads this and tries to reach me, she must do so with caution, as she will be watched by all parties, for the reason that she knows.

Contact: 1321-382-218, x110914."

Mr Veech's words seem spoken. Behind them I hear my uncle Dennis and Mr Rummage. I hope that they are safe, somewhere beneath the vaults of Burnchester. If anyone can find a route out it is they. Mr Veech may be in danger from our security people as well as the enemy. He seems still a free agent. I am grateful, and I must contact him.

I look for a report of the attack on Shingle Island. I can find nothing. It happened days ago, though it lives with me like yesterday. Is it possible that it has been kept secret, or even that they do not know? An idea hits me.

If nobody knows and Veech is the only man on the ground, it is my duty to let the authorities know what I have seen, whatever the risks. Somehow I must reach the highest authority in the land and report what I have seen. I must tell the Prime Minister.

The figure is looking at me from across the road.

I look again at the article. It is as if I am reading about another place, another life.

Only now does the reality hit me. This was my school. I was there. Where are my mother, my friends, Dennis, all of them? What has happened? Are they still alive?

I must find them. I want to scream. I cannot. I have been told to go on. I want to die. No. I will fight. I will carry on. I will find a way, through the dark tunnel, I must believe, I must have faith, even though I no longer know. I never did know. I am too young. I want to play again in the garden of my childhood and create my own dreams. I no longer have the props of belief, to help me on my way. My little cross-sword has long gone. Crushed under foot. My closest friends are gone. I no longer have my old self. I no longer believe.

Yet a new determination drives me on and a calm. I will use guile.

I turn down an alley and follow it until it joins a larger

street. I mix with shoppers, pause at a window, move on again.

There are police and security guards everywhere. And cameras. Like at Burnchester, only a hundred times worse.

I want to return there. But I cannot. I will at least find Mr Veech. Tell him what I know. What do I know, that he doesn't? That there is a mystery and a journey and a Dark Master and enemies seeking the knowledge that I, of all people, have been asked to carry, or is it something else? He would laugh at me. Except of course about Shingle Island. He could not laugh at that. I was there. I saw.... the Death Master.... tears form in my eyes.

I look for a phone box.

If Mr Veech did escape, perhaps others have escaped too? I feel better. I will find a library, plan my journey. I will find Mr Veech.

Perhaps my mother escaped and will find me. I think of Jess and Rick, and of the dark enemy who took them. I cannot bear to think of it.

I see their faces in the waves and begin to cry. I think of the distant Tom and my heart sinks. Tom, silent Tom, not seen since the night of – what shall I call it – the night of our "flight". Of course it didn't really happen. I remember it as if it did. And secretly, I still seek other ways. My mind has not been trained, but I will try again. It is one of the reasons we were there. At that school. The training that my uncle talked about. The training that they used – some of them used – to fight the enemy with all its power.

I try to follow the thought. What does it do, this power, if, that is, it isn't literally true? Suppose that we did not fly; but it felt as if it had happened, in our imagination so to speak, so true that it might have happened. As if we could fly with our eyes and imaginations and see as if we were there. That would be a start. We could see where no-one else could go, including behind enemy lines. I chose to forget that my

9

mother and Dennis had seen us in the sky, or so they thought. No, they saw us in the sky. Even PC Relish did.

Like that slow flash that first gave me the idea of returning to Burnchester – the description that so annoyed Jess – I realise something for the first time. All those visits to the tunnels, the conversations with Mr Rummage, the lessons with Mr Baxter and all our teachers, especially about masks, were part of something deeper. There was a hidden message all the time. Perhaps I have learned more than I thought, without knowing much. Deo Concedente. Perhaps I can fly with my mind. What else would it give me? The ability to travel with my mind's eye. I am not sure how I should try, but I will.

A small boy stands outside a shop, begging. I have little to give him. Nothing of value. I smile in sad acknowledgement. He looks at me blankly. It is like a spear in my heart. I struggle to find any change. I touch a last coin at the bottom of my bag. I put it in his hands.

A policeman comes up to the boy and tries to move him on. The boy stands and stares. I turn back and take his hand. I lead him into a cafe and ask the owner to give him something to eat. The man looks at me angrily, then points to the table. I lead the boy and sit him down.

The boy looks at me blankly. I kiss his cheek. I thank the man, and am about to leave. The man reminds me of the figure in the picture in the church. Why would he be angry then? Is he angry at me? I ask him if he can give me some change to phone my mother, as I am lost. He is angrier now.

As I walk past the cafe window, I look in and see the boy looking up. I try to cover my eyes. I feel certain that he smiles. He has the coin in his hand. He runs out and gives it to me.

Down the road there is a small crowd outside a shop. Three policemen are arguing with some young men. As I pass them, I tell the policemen to leave them alone. I have forgotten my promise not to get involved. I had forgotten the vigilantes. Fortunately they ignore me.

The man is following me again, on the other side of the road. I will try to lose him.

I am dizzy from hunger and tiredness, but my mind does not stop. Once I have contacted Mr Veech, I will make my way to Downing Street, and tell the Prime Minister. Then my secret will be safe, and I can disappear. Yet I doubt my idea already. I remember Mr Rummage's phrase, "above top secret". Perhaps the secret of the Spearhead, and now the Cell, must be preserved, even from him. I think of the phrase, "Hidden Energy; Secret Power".

I hear shouting and laughter. I turn round.

The boys are pointing at me. I do not know why.

I ignore them, and move on.

Now I am overwhelmed by guilt – at the thought of those I have left behind. And of fear for them. Of my mother, and my friends, and all the memories of happiness that gave me strength before my foolish return to the school. It is my fault. Even the little boy I could not give much money to. Why should I survive?

Where did I go wrong, why have I failed so abysmally to continue my journey, which I thought would be so easy? Where is that old adventure, where is the thrill of innocent life? It is somewhere with the child that I have left behind. The child of me. I do not believe. If there is an attack at Burnchester, they will all be killed.

Why should I survive? I can only hope Mr Rummage has led them to safety. But the dark figures are there too. What chance does he have against them? Yet he saved us once. And the cries from the fire. Is it to be repeated again, the bigotry and intolerance? By policemen doing an impossible job, questioning thousands of innocent people, in the hope of arresting a few?

The events of Shingle Island come at me again. The evil

canisters coming ashore. The sailor who warned us, now crucified. The figures overwhelming our forces. The woman who spoke to me, saved me from the pit.

How can I believe with all the suffering and the random pain? My old cross-sword lost in the pyre of the burning church. I miss its magical charm, the power that it seemed to instil, the gift of initiating change, through my imagination. Yet I know that I must leave it behind forever and pray – yes pray – that some other image will fill its place.

You, dear reader, if you still believe in those old symbols, do not accuse me of blasphemy, for sometimes I accuse myself. Are we not all flawed? Can we not only search for the thing that has meaning for us alone, as long as it does not harm others or oneself, and can be brought into communion with the beliefs of others? It is always, Deo Concedente. But who is Deus?

I run on, but my strength is failing. My task beckons through my despair. This solitude has a purpose, I was told. It is necessary. I remember the rising level of the sea. I must be careful not to be taken, not to be taken again, against my will, into the region below, again, beneath the waves, to recognise the instruments of darkness for what they are, not what I imagine them to be. I must see through false hope, but recognise the light, and fight for the truth. Not be consumed by despair.

I long to see Jess and Rick. I think of Tom's words: "There are many ways to fly". I think of my mother and my father. The tears fall down my face.

An image comes into my mind, as yet a blur. Struggling to be born. And with it comes new energy, new hope, just there, enough to bring me back and lead me on. I laugh at what I have experienced of the dark. I have been initiated. Nothing can stop me now. Nothing can change my mind. But I must act with stealth, not just fortitude. The enemy is subtle, often hidden. Keep watch, and trust your ability to judge. The journey from light to dark and into light is endless, for all time. Many births and deaths, but always resurrection. "Be innocent of the knowledge dearest chuck."

I am compelled, against my conscious will, towards the crossing point between energy and power.

My forehead has begun to bleed again.

A helicopter passes overhead.

I see a telephone kiosk. I check the number at the bottom of the article, lift the receiver and dial. It is an unusual number. Engaged.

People pass the kiosk, all extraordinary, following the paths given to them, or forged by themselves in a dance between personality, circumstance and fate. Many races, many cultures, every age, every faith. The past is here – especially the past is here, seeking recognition for its unfulfilled work – and the future too. Generations from outside time, keep watch and ward, ever about to be. Poor and poorer, rich and rich enough. Humanity in our own city. Children laughing, children lying. The torment of rejection, the creativity of love. The rage of youth and the rage and beauty of age. Violence and peace, the light and the dark, forever struggling to restore humanity to its possibilities, by eternal struggle. Is it no more than "only the trying"? The search for the essence of it all. Laughter, sadness, folly. The struggle forward, ever onward and upward. What can we all do?

Bear witness and go forward. Better than that. Seek the beginning from which all our futures are told. Find the meaning of the Sacred Cell, and let it grow on the hill of paradise.

"Who is this please?" says a voice.

"I want to leave a message for Mr Veech."

There are security people by a shop opposite, outside the Job Centre, by the entrances to the bank and pub. The sound of sirens comes in waves, like the echo of a sea-swamped bell. Unreal City.

"Who is this?"

"I have an urgent message for Mr Veech. Tell him...."

The face is watching me from the other side of the road. There are now two of them. I have a horror that I will be taken. I thought my disguise was perfect. Have they recognised me?

I am short of breath, and try to speak slowly.

"Please. I know Mr Veech. Mr name is.... I cannot say it. Tyro. I am connected to the school, the one he wrote about in the paper. He knows my mother and my head teacher. It is important that I see him. I must see him. I have information about the Island. Please. How can I find him? Please hurry."

"How do I spell that?"

"Where can I reach him? No.... I have no mobile, no phone, does he have an email? Does he have a direct line? Where is he?"

"He is on an assignment at the moment. He cannot be reached by phone directly. There is no active email address. I cannot give his contact details out I'm afraid. Can you ring back? Can we ring you? What is your number?"

I have no chance to reply. The phone goes dead, as if the woman had been asked to end the conversation.

I hasten on until I am out of sight of the figures, and the security. Down a side alley. I'll find a library. Then head for the centre of town, and find a way, any way, of entering Number 10.

I can feel the gentle trickle of blood on my forehead. I lean against a wall.

A boy comes over from the other side of the road.

"You need a doctor."

I shake my head and straighten. I feel for the cell about my body.

"I'm OK."

I avoid looking into the boy's face, yet I sense that it is warm. I am reminded of Ali from school.

He moves his leg as if he is in pain.

14

My heart beats faster. I blush, but he cannot see because of my disguise.

"It's you who needs help."

"We can help each other then," he says.

He takes my hand while I steady myself.

His touch gives me strength. Something comes back to me. Some image passes before me as a ghost, a retrieval, like a memory. Perhaps it is nothing.

"I'll find bandages."

"No. I must find a library. I need some information. Then...."

The boy sees the two figures, watching.

"Who....?" he whispers.

"They've been following me. I thought I'd lost them. It's me they're after."

"Follow me," he says.

# 2

The large man in a suit enters a door at the top of the tallest City tower. Mr Blakemore and Mr Vespers follow, their prisoner between them.

The door closes. A guard stands outside.

The large man turns to the prisoner.

"Please sit down."

The prisoner does not move.

The suited man turns towards the window.

We see a magnificent view. Spirals of cloud hang from an adjacent tower.

In the distance, the cathedral of St Pauls. Beyond, the Houses of Parliament and the Abbey Church of St Peter the Great. Far below, the river, whose waters are rising.

On a set of screens to the right of the window are pictures of other cities across the world: New York; Shanghai; Mumbai; Tokyo; Moscow.

The prisoner takes in everything.

The penthouse is modern, much of it high-tech, but here and there are other, older signs.

There are framed documents, pictures of medieval paintings on two walls. There is a replica of the triptych in the church of St Mary Magdalene. A representation of a spearhead.

This seems to change shape. The prisoner wonders if it does so according to who is looking at it, and when, or why.

There is a picture of a mansion in East Anglia. The prisoner recognises where he, Inspector Relish, Dennis, and Rick, watched Mr Strangelblood and the Stranger on that distant night.

Mr Strangelblood, for surely it is he, knows as well as any what is happening at Burnchester.

On the floor in front of him is a circular stone with a chair in front of it.

The prisoner is directed to it, but he does not move. His expression is unchanged. Shadows are his business.

Mr Strangelblood is on the phone.

"The Chamber guarded?.... Satisfactory. No-one can enter or exit?.... The Dr, no doubt, will advise us. Shingle Island? Satisfactory.

If necessary take them both. Then head north. After we have taken Doonwreath, the girl will do the rest, assuming she has the object. And then...."

The prisoner has heard of the secret station in the Highlands. Central to Mr Rummage's plan. On no account must it fall.

*

I and the boy hurry along the high road.

Two police cars cruise past, followed by an ambulance.

The traffic moves sideways. A horn. Someone is nearly hit. Other police cars appear.

I wipe my brow. Something scrapes against my skin, something hard. The cell is wrapped inside my handkerchief, which I took from my back pocket. There is a dull smudge over the gash.

"Why so many police?"

"There's going to be trouble. A lot of trouble. Nobody is safe."

"Why?"

We turn down a side street.

"Hang on a minute. Wait!"

I hold the boy back. He looks at the mess I have made of my face, which I try to hide.

His expression changes. I feel disconcerted. His face returns almost to its former look, shadowed by something else, watching. It is as if he no longer trusts me.

"I was OK before you came along. I don't want help. I'm going on alone."

I turn away.

I see two men that look like security guards, asking questions. They have appeared from nowhere. One of them mentions a girl. The other looks at me. I turn my head.

"There's a pharmacy in the next street," the boy says.

"I don't care. Leave me alone!"

"Listen!" the boy shouts, holding me by the shoulders. "There's trouble already and there's going to be more. Didn't you see those two? They might have taken you or me. They're working for them. They were not ordinary police."

"What are you talking about?"

"Haven't you heard? On the news this morning. There's a State of Emergency."

"A what?"

"Because of what's happening. First, that school. Now a secret military establishment – some island somewhere – has been taken over, by an unknown force – though they try to hush it up, and they are at the end of their tether. There's talk of an invasion, but of what nobody knows. People are taken in and questioned, but some are by gangs with other agendas. People disappear.

On top of it all, the Thames has begun to flood. The fact is, nobody knows what is behind it all."

"How do you know all this?"

He points to my paper.

"I read and listen and watch. You have to. My father was

taken and I want to find him. I have to be careful. He was being watched."

I look at him questioningly.

"People say it is terrorist infiltration. The Priory is just a cover. But they are not clear. The matter of what happened at that school, is more than that. It is about power. Secret Power. The power of the universe. Seems as if the army's about to blast their way in. A lot of good that will do. I should know. And then there's the rest. Where do you think I got this?"

I look at his leg.

"Interrogation. They stop anyone. Some are looking for drugs and guns, others for terrorists. Terrorist cells. But there's something else. There's this constant talk of secret infiltration, even a virus."

"A virus?" It was a word Mr Rummage used.

We are in a road lined with a few small shops. Like something out of one of those old Mediterranean towns.

"I'm sorry.... I was impatient. I'm exhausted. Why did you stop back there and look at me so strangely?"

The boy ignores me, tells me to keep a look out while he goes into a shop.

I watch passers-by reflected in the window. I like him, but I must not, cannot be, slowed down. I have to act quickly. Two is not always better than one. Yet I am curious. What did he mean by, "I should know?"

The boy comes out of the shop, carrying something.

"He says you can clean up inside. Take these bandages. He's a friend of mine."

"How do I know I can trust you?"

"I didn't ask to be trusted."

"But...." I stop short.

"You said it's you they're after didn't you? That makes two of us."

He keeps a look out, while I enter the shop.

The man shows me into the back, where there is a wash

room. Why is the boy looking after me? What does he want? I calm, saying it is nothing, nothing but what is in me.

The boy's face is looking at me, as if it is in the mirror, perhaps behind the mirror, the face of almost recognition. And there are many layers to it, from different places, coming at me as if by day, then by night, in the church, along the road.

Then suddenly, I stare in horror at what I see. The blood on my forehead has dried into the shape of a symbol. A symbol that I know. The symbol of the Priory. I am horrified.

I try to rub it out. I put on some cream, ignoring the bandage.

As I leave the shop, the man picks up the phone and dials.

The boy and I walk on.

I will leave him soon, though I am curious.

"What's your name?" I ask.

"They call me Jolly."

I try not to laugh.

"Mine's.... Jess."

The boy suggests we go to a cafe. He has another friend who owes him. I like him. I think he knows it. I tell him that I have to leave soon.

We hear more sirens. I take the boy's arm and tap his leg. This time he does smile, and not in pain.

"What happened?"

"I told you, interrogation."

There are several people in the cafe. There is a television in the corner.

I go to a table out of sight of the entrance. My head nearly falls into my hands from tiredness.

The boy comes over with sandwiches and tea.

"Is there a back door?" I ask, turning. "In case I have to make a quick exit. Thanks."

The boy leans over to me.

"You're from that school aren't you?"

"What sort of interrogation?"

"They hurt me. But I gave them nothing. About me. About my father. Then I escaped."

He continues.

"We have to trust each other. You said you need to find a library. I can take you."

I eat hurriedly and sip the tea – the warmth is wonderful. I hand the newspaper over, pointing to the name of Mr Veech.

"I want to contact him. I need information for my.... journey. I tried earlier, without success."

I begin to feel a presence in the cafe that I don't like.

I look about me. There are a few of the customers with their backs turned, one of whom is a man wearing a coat. I imagine the hinted etching of a cross-sword, like a corrupted Templar Knight. I start to choke.

The man gets up to pay. His face becomes visible.

"I want to find out about a place called Doonwreath. Tell me about you? By the way, my name's not Jess."

The boy takes a moment to react.

"It started some months ago, with that weird business in the school, as I said. There was a lot in the press. Secret societies, threats to the church, to the state. Talk about a sacred object of great power, capable of destroying us all.

Then there was the death of the Bishop, which some said was linked.

Then there was this Shingle Island business. Hushed up of course, but bad. Nobody really knows."

I sip my tea.

"Meanwhile different groups have been carrying out acts of their own, in the name of different causes. A kind of gang war, but not in the normal sense. Not just local. Violence, vigilante groups, more violence, police, people taken in and held without charge. A darkening landscape.

A state of emergency.

They've lost control. It's something bigger, this virus. No-one will say what. Except that it's very big. There's threats

21

from everywhere. Everyone blames everyone else. There's even talk of the end of time."

"The end of time! That's ridiculous! And no panic?"

"Not yet. People have enough on their plate trying to survive. There's still people with big cars, big houses. In a way I feel most sorry for them. Most to lose. Most deluded. Will cling on 'till the end. There are more and more kids on the streets too. Like me. Like us. Police can't cope. Some have no parents – too busy for them even to look. But now people are having to listen. Now the Thames is about to drown us all."

"Why aren't people demanding to know?"

"They won't tell you. Life's too difficult, too short. We've been at war around the world for too long already. Without good cause. Just up the ante. What difference will it make, to know? Besides, they're fed up with it. It's kind of unreal. Like the plague. Doesn't exist until it hits you.

Then there's fear. Some people do want to know, of course. Seek the truth. But they tend to get silenced. Like my father. But now it's different. And it may be too late. Anyway, the government loves to talk up fear. Excuses anything. But they don't know."

"Slowly the poison the whole bloodstream fills."

The boy looks at me.

"The line of a poem. My English teacher loved poetry, especially Shakespeare."

It's like an admission.

Something about the boy connects. I know I have seen him before.

"Sad. That wasn't Shakespeare."

I begin to sense what Mr Rummage was hinting at, about the virus spreading. I wished I had asked him more. Why didn't I ask him about my father's work? Mum never told me much. Mr Rummage's instructions were clear. Head north.

Never stop until there is no further to climb, and then it is your chance to reach the stars. I think of the school. In the distance now. Not an ordinary place, is it? Not like normal schools that people go to. It had another effect. Like chanting in the bones. Like music in the blood. No doubt there was some very practical training to be done, for those old soldiers who still haunt the place. Survival, mental discipline, counter-interrogation techniques, methods of killing the enemy. But there was a deeper thing going on, another level of initiation. To do with the Power. The Energy. The place in-between. The stream below. I think of my father.

Things come back to me. Memories, scenes, sounds, smells, in moments of broken light, outside time. I recall seeing the landscape from a great height, in the moon-filled darkness: the entirety of space before me, with the freedom to move across the night sky, yet controlled by my intuitions. I begin to wonder if this wasn't a hint, a glimpse of what we were trying to achieve. I had a sense, but lacked the insight.

I feel it is to do with the ability to travel in time and place, though how this relates to the cell I do not know. I recall the instructions that we copied from the library, in the old script, that might have been Shakespeare.

"Only in combination can these powers be used effectively.... they will only function in combination with energy from other sources."

Our journey at sea comes back to me:

The sight of the ancient city, the old ship, the visit to the arena, the terror of the bodies lying across the beach, and the storm that took Rick and Jess, and allowed me to escape. I remember my first arrival back on land. I remember my descent into the depths.

I think of the picture that Miss Peverell showed us in the class, before the invasion. I called it the Sick Eagle. I remember the path, hidden beneath the avenue of trees, appearing in gaps in the leaves. It led towards the castle in the distance, at the top of a hill; except that in the dead ground out of sight, there was something we couldn't see.

I remember the box of childish things under my bed. I blush. For one particular image lying there. I recall my lost innocence, like in that other poem.

I see the picture on my wall at home, with blood streaming down my face, and the horizon, and remember the empty frame in the church. And it is upon this which my mind rests. The empty frame. How do the images come? From where? When?

"Are you sure we're safe here?" I ask.

"Yes."

I look at the boy.

"The enemy. Government forces or the Priory. Whoever seeks control. The true enemy, the power behind the chaos, is always invisible. Sometimes it's hard to tell who is working for whom. There are other groups too, who say they are the police, plain clothes. Carry identity cards. But nobody knows for sure."

Our eyes connect. I am about to speak, when I see panic in his eyes, and he tries to continue, but I interrupt him.

"What did you mean by "I should know"? And your father? What happened to him?"

The boy's caution is obvious.

"You know?"

"Something else is bothering you. Tell me."

"We may not meet again."

The boy touches my face. I feel his soft touch, his soft skin against mine. He takes my hand and places my fingers on the cut. The skin is smooth.

"The cut has gone, but there is something else," the boy says. I look towards the cafe window.

I lift my hand, with a kind of fear. My skin is intact.

But something else remains. I lean closer to the window.

The blood that I had wiped with my handkerchief, that

I cleaned in the shop, is now a brown smudge, though the incision has gone. Yet the brown smudge, which I had wiped with the hidden cell, forms a shape, like a shallow relief on my forehead. It is in the shape of something familiar. It is an insignia of some sort.

My face goes white. I try to feel the colour. The boy smiles at me innocently, yet there is a shock of recognition too, which I feel he is trying to deny. The insignia has gone, and my face is clean.

"What does it mean?"

"It was a sign."

"Of what?"

"I do not know."

# 3

Close to the Houses of Parliament and the great Abbey Church, the Head of the Security Service, MI5, sits at a table in Thames House. She may be tense, though her face reveals nothing. The room is well lit. The walls are heavily sound-proofed. This is a secure room.

There are four others present: the Home Secretary; the Head of the Secret Intelligence Service, MI6; the Head of the Joint Chiefs of the Defence Staff and the Prime Minister.

"Nothing from Rummage, nothing from Relish, nothing from any of them? What happened to those secret escape routes? I thought we had a journalist embedded?"

The Head of the Intelligence Service answers in a factual, steady tone – without concealing the gathering clouds.

"Special Forces have reached an impenetrable barrier in the tunnels, and there is no news of any of the people. No contact. It's as if they've disappeared. Including Veech."

"It's a shambles. The most sophisticated technology in the world at our disposal and we can do nothing."

The Prime Minister intervenes.

"What do you propose, Joint Chief?"

"We have done what we can, Prime Minister. Our Special Forces have tried to break in. The RAF has tried an aerial attack, but cannot pass over the dome. Our last chance is a full frontal ground assault. There is no certainty we will succeed. We await the order, Prime Minister. And there will be consequences."

The Home Secretary speaks:

"We have lost an entire school. All the children, all the parents, all staff; never mind our undercover people, the military and the police officers. And we do not know why. It's lucky people haven't taken to the streets."

"They have, Sir."

The group turn towards a screen on the wall, which has multiple elements.

They see various shots of the area around Burnchester Hall: the driveway to the entrance; the Church; the river Dean; the main school. There is no sign of life. There are the charred remains of a fire, the remains of one of the buildings.

Outside the grounds, people have formed a camp which is growing by the minute. Some are holding placards. One reads, "Find our children."

There are television crews from around the world, standing at every point of access to the school. The military struggles to keep them back.

An aerial shot from a police helicopter shows the surrounding countryside: road blocks on the small country routes; local people trying to get through; people being turned away.

We can see the Burnchester Arms, which is overflowing with people, the car-park full. There are boats along the river.

Higher still, we look out across the east coast and pick up the familiar skyline around Dunemoor, and Southwold. Out to sea, is a flotilla of naval vessels. On the beach, a group of people search the shoreline.

The Head of MI5 speaks next.

"If you look towards the horizon, you will see the southern tip of Shingle Island. We have surrounded it, but cannot get close. An area three miles inland is also impenetrable."

"What can be done?"

"We know that a girl called Tyro escaped with two friends. She is under observation. She may be our only hope."

"One girl against this?" The Home Secretary is used to the fantasies of his colleagues.

"It seems that she holds something of great importance."

She looks at the Head of MI6.

"Meanwhile, the river has broken its banks and we have an emergency alert. People are demanding answers, and action. We have lost all contact with Shingle Island support station and cannot get close to it either. The threats are increasing. There is a serious threat of disintegration. The line is only just being held. Evacuation procedures are in place. We only have to give the order."

"Do we know who is behind this?"

"We think it is led by a small group called the Priory, searching for an object of great power. But the stakes have risen, and the forces now are multiple."

"And what does that mean?"

"It means we do not know, Sir."

"Do not know? The best surveillance equipment known to humankind, the greatest resources for monitoring in the Western hemisphere and we do not know!"

"Whatever it is, is profound evil."

The Head of MI6 continues:

"Our foreign agents tell us there have been similar incidents in the US, Russia, and China, and that they are growing by the day."

"The Church is demanding information – in a very unchristian way, I'm told."

"We have been contacted by friendly countries and not so friendly countries to ask what's going on – it seems they think we are responsible – but we're unable to tell them anything. We can't even put a spin on it."

"Who the hell are these guys?"

There is a pause. Outside a siren sounds in the distance. It is a long drawn out wail. Reminiscent of the Blitz.

The Home Secretary turns to his colleagues.

"I want information – and I want it now. Do whatever it takes. I want you to find the girl, this Tyro, and bring her in. We can't wait for possibilities, or for the enemy to get to her first. I cannot believe that she holds the future in her hands."

"It may be more serious than you think, Prime Minister."

"Why?"

"The enemy is watching her too. If we take her, we may lose a chance to get to them."

"I want an update on all our allies and enemies. I want you to find someone close to Mr Rummage. Somebody must know. And I don't want to see you again until you have something positive to report."

The Head of MI5 answers.

"There are things above top secret, Home Secretary, that nobody is supposed to know. I think we may be in that very territory now."

"Above Top Secret! What is that supposed to mean?"

"That the search is on, for the Hidden Universe: the Secret Power. If it gets completely lost, we are finished. We are dealing with a force outside our control."

"Nothing is above top secret anymore. See that lot on the beach?"

The Home Secretary points to the picture of the men searching.

"They're searching for barrels. Barrels of the most toxic substance known to man. Washed up. Nobody knows where from."

The Head of MI5 looks at his superior.

"It wasn't only the children who escaped the Dome, Home Secretary. Three others did as well. Three of the Priory, we think, who have been accused of the Bishop's murder."

"Find them, Director. Find them. Before it is too late. For them. For us. For us all."

The Prime Minister storms out. He is followed by the Home Secretary, and the Joint Chief. The Heads of MI5 and MI6 exchange glances.

*

Mr Strangelblood replaces the receiver and turns to a map of the world.

Surrounding it, across the wall, is an image of the solar system. First we see our galaxy, then, as the picture grows, we see reflections of distant galaxies. What is extraordinary is that the image is alive, and moving subtly, as if it was a picture of actual space, which is what it is. There are explosions and changes in energy intensity here and there; meteors pass, the whole is more than three dimensional, and appears infinitely complex. A series of worlds at once adjacent then folding into one another, first clear, bright and distinct, then apparently rolled into one.

The entire wall is like a projection of the universe.

As we look into it we become lost in the eternity of space. Newton might have glimpsed such a view through the vertical telescope at Burnchester.

Mr Strangelblood turns to the prisoner.

"Soon this will be ours too. Dr Bartok."

"A little presumptuous, isn't it, to think you can possess the universe?"

"The London extension of your Dream Notation Chamber is under observation. The girl will be taken to it. Neither they, nor we, can progress without the information she can give. You will assist us. We are relying on your knowledge. You understand the language of the mind Dr Bartok. It is in your interests to co-operate. We need to make use of it. The energy required. Where it will lead. Especially any sign of messages from.... afar."

"What have you done with the parchment?" Dr Bartok asks.

30

"My, how shall we say, junior colleague has done a deal with the Church. The information it contains is to be checked by a small working party, some of our people, two of theirs. If what the parchment reveals is true, they will have no choice but to co-operate – for as long as we need them. And then.... when the "object" bears fruit, they will no longer be needed.

The world, not just the hordes of the dead, who are desperate to return, will come to us. The Church's power will be lost. Ours will be infinite."

Dr Bartok doesn't react.

"And what about the forces of the State? You have a history Mr Strangelblood."

Mr Strangelblood is silent.

Dr Bartok continues.

"And the Americans, the Chinese, the Russians? Do you think they will let you get away with this?"

"We, including you and your distinguished colleagues, have the knowledge and the expertise to access powers, in conjunction with the "object", greater than all others in our world. They can't compete. Perhaps you would like to join us Dr Bartok?"

Dr Bartok glances towards the window.

"I will then be a seen as a saviour. Not bad to be thought of as a new Messiah."

Mr Strangelblood looks into Dr Bartok's eyes. Dr Bartok is looking at the images of the universe. On the screen he can frame his own images and occasionally meet others' there; as yet unborn from a future of infinite space.

Dr Bartok speaks softly, as if to himself.

"I have no spur
To prick the sides of my intent, but only
Vaulting ambition, which o'erleaps itself
And falls on th'other."

The hint of a smile appears on Mr Strangelblood's face.

"Shakespeare, of course, was known to me. I may even be said to have helped him from time to time."

"You are long-lived Mr.... I'm sorry I have forgotten your name. Mephistopheles, perhaps."

There is a pause. The guards look anxiously for Mr Strangelblood's anger.

"A mere literary device!"

Mr Strangelblood turns and looks towards the Houses of Parliament.

There is a call. An assistant answers.

"Someone from the Cabinet Office, Sir. He did not give a name. Something to do with counter-intelligence."

"I am not available."

"He says it is a matter of the greatest importance."

Mr Strangelblood turns. He is shaking with fury.

"Imbecile! I told you, I am not available."

One of his advisers edges forward.

"Perhaps it would be advisable...." but Mr Strangelblood waves him aside.

He knows that they have an extensive file on him. Most of it lies. Misinformation and smokescreen, but their tentacles are deep and almost as old as his. However, their relationship to power is more equivocal. And he has been useful to them. They, after all, use his services in their training from time to time. The Prime Minister may need him.

"Take Dr Bartok away. You know where."

For the first time in the meeting, Dr Bartok goes over to Mr Strangelblood, and looks him in the eye.

"Shakespeare might have loved equivocation, but he always sides with the right in the end."

Mr Strangelblood places his hand over the speaker on his desk.

"In the end there is only me."

*

32

I am troubled by the symbol. The shadowy Order of the Magdalene comes to mind, for that is whose I think it was.

I notice a security camera trained on the door.

"You've come a long way, haven't you," the boy says.

I point to my rucsac, but he shakes his head.

"No. I know you. I didn't always live in the city. You said your name wasn't Jess."

The boy glances up at the proprietor. He sees that I see. His face tenses. Another CCTV camera faces us from the corner.

"Don't worry. He owes me. I saved him a lot of trouble once. I think things are moving steadily towards a head."

"You said...."

He pauses.

*

It is now that my own past begins to unravel. The past held from me by the death of my father, in some corner of time. There, I have said it. I have used the words that I never wished to acknowledge, hoping beyond hope that he would come back and tell me stories again. But it is not possible. Here in the dark corner of the city, I recognise for the first time that my parents are truly no longer there, the father who has died, and the mother who has disappeared. I am alone. I am more angry than I can explain. If only.... And yet there is sad relief too, in being free.

*

The boy's face is transfixed. I follow his gaze. Two figures are watching from outside.

One of them walks towards the door. The other towards the cafe window.

"Time to leave," I whisper.

"Go by the back door. I'll go to the counter. Delay him."

33

The figure at the window seems to scan the whole of the interior. He sees the CCTV camera pointing at our table.

Its eyes follows the line to where I was sitting.

The second figure enters the cafe and stands behind my friend.

My pulse is beginning to race. Shall I leave now?

I look at the face at the window, but it is partly hidden. A horrible feeling pervades the air, as if nature has been silenced.

I follow the figure's movements. It turns towards the alley at the side of the cafe. I seek his reflection in the window. There is no reflection there.

My limbs freeze in horror. I check again, expecting to see in the half-light of the shaded front, the imprint of a man's outline in the glass.

I feel the blood drain from my face, leaving me like a death mask. Where the image of the figure should have been, there is something else.

A hollow frame moves stealthily from side to side, like a tree in the wind. The image of a monk-like figure dressed in a cloak, standing head down, a broad red cross-sword across its back. Except that in this case there is blood falling from the sword's limbs.

I am near to collapse. I try to call out, but there is no sound. I crash into the table, sending it sideways. I fall but scramble up, and try to call again. The boy runs over. The second figure tries to stop him, screaming at the top of his voice.

"Seize that girl! I will pay you any money you want to stop her escaping. Stop her in the name of the....!"

The boy turns and blocks the figure. With the cafe owner they try to bring it to the ground, but it shrugs them off with a will and an ease that is unearthly and unstoppable.

The boy tries to reach the back exit, but the figure throws him to the ground. The figure then turns to the cafe owner and stills him with one blow. He then runs out after me, who he sees standing at the alley exit, in front of the other figure, waiting to ensnare me. The boy runs out behind the second figure, badly hurt.

Just as the first figure tries to bring me down from behind, my friend screams out to warn me.

I find the strength to remain still. I decide on another approach. I could try flight, but I am not sure that I have that skill, and that would be cowardly. I could try guile, but I am too straightforward yet. I could try strength, but I alone do not possess it. I need the power from something else, and if my journey is what I am told it is, I should have that if the moment is right. And if it isn't, I shall be a captive, though I will fight in every way I can.

The figure behind me has stopped while the other stands in front of me, leaving a space through which I can pass into the street, as if to hint that I might go forward unharmed. I suspect they have a plan.

Inside my pocket I gradually uncurl the blood-rimmed handkerchief that clasps the cell. I concentrate and try to draw down the energy as once I felt I could, though I am still unpractised in the art.

Concentrating hard, I hold the object in my hand which I bring forward.

I sense the shape of something emerge from my hand, like a lance or spear, the head of which is the object, though it now shines brightly with strange power, and has a subtly new shape. Its sides are razor sharp. I am afraid of the power it gives out, imagining that it could be used against me.

The figures stop in their tracks. Against their will, they move away, but only by the force of what I hold. They would continue if they could. They seem to see the spear and watch it carefully, at one time holding out a crumpled arm to take it, but in vain. I feel sure that the boy can't see it. Yet he sees the figures' reaction.

With my free hand I take the boy's arm, and together we

walk down the alley and out into the street. He is confused but he follows my instructions.

In moments we are free, and begin to run. The figures are behind, but do not come too close. The spear has gone and the object is back in my hand. I replace it in my back pocket.

Outside the cafe a crowd has gathered, headed by the boy's friend. They seem to be bewildered by what has happened, and yet it is not clear what they can see.

I let go of the boy's arm. We continue along the back streets, turning suddenly here and there, to try and lose the figures.

"Who were they?"

"They've been following me.... from the beginning. You saw them earlier. I think they work for the Priory, but I am not sure. One of them, the one who tried to stop me, is known as the Stranger and I think is their leader. He seems to come from another world."

"Whoever they are, that was impressive."

I look at him.

"The way you got rid of them. I thought we were going to have to fight it out. How did you do it? People were amazed."

"I'll tell you one day. Did you see?"

"See what?"

"The help that I had."

"No. A weapon?"

"Kind of."

The boy doesn't react.

We weave in and out of the small streets and alleys that make up this part of the old city. We keep our eyes open for the figures. When we get to a main street, we jump on a bus. We go to the top deck. The boy looks at me, anxiously.

"You're Tyro, aren't you?"

I do not react.

"Tell me what happened to your father."

The boy looks ahead.

"My father was taken.... I don't know where. There are

others who have disappeared, taken by unknown groups. Nobody knows where. Nobody can find out. It is as if they are blanked off the face of the earth. The police are out of control. It even happened in my school."

"Before you continue. I want to say something." I look at him. "Will you not ask me too many questions? Not yet."

He stares at me.

"My father is dead."

"I'm sorry."

I see my tears in his eyes.

"Go on."

"As I told you, there are groups, often in plain clothes, who say that they are police. Carry identity cards. But nobody knows for sure. The police deny any of it is them, of course. People are taken away for questioning. We don't know why. One of them was my father. I haven't seen him since it happened. I get no answers. It sounds far-fetched, but people think that someone has taken them over, or is trying to. Everyone has a price."

"Why was he taken?"

"My father worked on a secret project."

"Worked?"

"Works, then. Except that.... well, I fear the worst. None of us knew what it was, or even that he was. But his behaviour suggested it. He couldn't even tell his family. He wasn't even supposed to say that it was secret. But we knew. He tried to use a cover, but it didn't work. The cracks in his story appeared, and then we suspected, though my mother first thought it was something else. He was carrying a burden. Of knowing. He became unhappy. He wanted to talk. But he couldn't."

"What happened?"

"One day we confronted him. At least I did. My mother was listening. But he denied it, most of it anyway. All he said was, "I can't talk about it." This made my mother really angry. She screamed at him that if he couldn't talk about it to his wife and son, who the hell could he talk about it to? She broke down. He tried to calm her but she pushed him away.

We were used to it. Ever since I was a child he spoke in riddles, so this was to be expected. He used to say that life is like a code. Break the code and you will find the meaning, though the symbols are always changing. I kind of knew what he was trying to say. But it was only an impression. It made me want to find out more. I was going to ask him. Then he disappeared.

One day he left for work, as usual. Left his room and his study, as he usually did. Kissed my mum goodbye and shouted to me upstairs to be good, and closed the door. We haven't seen him since."

I put my hand on his arm. He turns towards me. His gentle eyes.

"What do you think his work was?"

The boy shakes his head. "I don't know."

"We tried to reach him but his phone was turned off; we tried his work numbers – we were only supposed to phone in an emergency – but they had no idea where he was. When my mother shouted down the phone that she demanded some action, they repeated that they had no idea where he might be, but that someone would come and see her and tell her what they knew. She's still waiting."

I thought of my own father. I don't even know where he is buried.

"My father...." I begin. I must learn to listen. My anger cannot always be my guide.

"....I'll tell you later."

"My mum feels really guilty. Now that he has gone. She cries all the time, which makes her feel worse."

"How long ago was this? What did you do?"

"At first I stayed to help my mother. But she told me not to. She is convinced that my father has been taken. When I asked who by, she shook her head, though I think she suspects. Maybe she is trying to protect me. I left the house, against my mother's entreaty, thinking I might be taken, though I go back in secret when I can.

My mother is still there. I feel I've abandoned her, but I had to choose. Yet I know my father wanted to tell me something. Something about what he was doing. Perhaps to re-assure me, or to warn me. I don't know. But the house is being watched, so I have to be careful."

The boy looks about him. His face looks older. A fear creeps over it.

"Was he in trouble with the police?"

"The people who took him left this. One day it was put through the letter box. And with it a letter. Here, read it. There's a strange invitation."

I stare at the object in disbelief. I notice the familiar insignia, the same that had been on the Neptune, and carved at the base of Gruff's injured body. That had been on my forehead. There is a pause. The atmosphere seems to have changed, not just between us.

"But why?"

"Perhaps it's like tempting us to follow. They can't return so they get us to come. I think they want information."

I tell him that I know what it's like to be hunted, to live in the shadows, waiting for the right moment to continue the journey. Or for a sign.

I ignore the letter.

I pick up the object and study it.

My face goes white. He asks me what the matter is.

"This," I say. "I've seen it before."

I take out the object I found on the beach at Shingle Island.

The boy stares, then picks it up. He is in a state of shock.

"Where did you get it? It is my father's!"

I put the object down, stunned.

Before I can answer, the boy looks about him. He grabs my

hand and leads me down the steps. We leap off the bus just before it stops.

We run into a crowded street market.

"What happened?" I ask.

"I got a feeling. We can't take risks," he says.

We approach a busy road.

There are several police close to a small demonstration. One of them is filming it. Two people carry a placard.

"Stop government secrecy! Answers now!"

There is angry shouting. Others stand by at first, then join the group.

A policeman watches from the back of a car.

Close to us is another small group. From it two figures emerge like shadows. They turn away as soon as they see us.

The officer in the car notices us.

We cross the road, but the demonstration blocks our path.

I sense a terrible energy. I hear whispers.

The crowd sense something is very wrong.

A police car pulls up alongside us. The window winds down.

"You there!"

The officer, who was filming the demonstration, is now filming us.

A policeman gets out of the car, tapping my friend in the back.

"You, son!"

"Lay off me!" He says, swinging round.

"What's your name?"

I point to the figures who are close by.

"They tried to kidnap us! You should arrest them."

The officer with the camera looks at the figures.

"Why aren't you in school?"

"It's none of your business."

"He didn't mean that," I say. "I tell you, these .... er.... people tried to kidnap us. There are witnesses."

The policeman points the camera at the boy's face.

"What's in the bag?"

"None of your business!"

"Ignore him officer. He doesn't mean any harm. He's often like this."

"What's this about being attacked?"

I clasp the cell. The policeman turns to face me.

"And you are, Miss?"

My friend snaps. He lunges at the policeman.

"You took my father! You bastards! Where is he? You're not policemen anyway!"

The policeman grabs his arm and pins him back.

"You're coming with me."

I try to intervene, but the boy tells me to run.

In the police car, an officer studies a photograph on the screen, then looks at me. Another set shows the faces of a young man.

I concentrate and hold the cell in my hand.

"We should take her in for questioning."

I scream out, pointing to the policeman next to the figures. His face is like a death mask.

The two policemen run to their colleague. The boy is thrown to the ground. The two figures block the policemen's way.

The policeman shouts at them to stand back. One holds up his gun.

The figures gradually lift their hands and arms, as the second policeman goes behind them.

"Arms behind your back! Not one move! Not one!"

There is a split-second pause. The gun is pointed at the head of one of the figures, who speaks slowly, deliberately.

"It's that girl you want!"

The policeman calls for reinforcements.

"I'm taking you all in! Hand-cuff those two! Then get in the car. You're under arrest."

I focus all my energies on the cell. I hope and pray.

Everything for a moment stops still.

Then it all happens at once. My arm lifts upwards and an overwhelming force projects from the cell, knocking the figures to the ground and stunning them. Their cloaks collapse like rag dolls. The policemen are blinded by the light and grope around helplessly.

People on the pavement fall back in amazement and horror, pointing and screaming, some turning away, others transfixed. The screaming increases and becomes the penetrating sound of an approaching siren.

We hear the crackle of voices over the intercom.

The policemen are regaining their sight.

Two more police vehicles break through the crowd of onlookers. The demonstrators see their chance.

"Let's go!" I say, backing away.

We run down a narrow side street.

"Who were they?"

"I don't know."

I feel a searing pain, like a spear has been thrust into my body. I stumble. The boy bends to help me up, touches my forehead. I move his hand away. Both his and mine are covered in blood.

"I'll be OK. Let's get away – as far as possible."

"They took my dad. They're not going to get me."

"They're not going to get either of us."

There is something about the boy which haunts me. I try to make the connection.

"That was impressive," the boys says.

"Let's find the library. Then we can leave the city."

"Wait here. I'll ask in the shop. I won't be long."

His eyes glitter as if from some far off place, yet they belong to our world too. They seem to be in pain but also reveal something else. Something that I lack.

As if from nowhere come Shakespeare's words:

"Full fathom five thy father lies,
Of his bones are coral made;
Those are pearls that were his eyes,
Nothing of him that doth fade
But doth suffer a sea-change
Into something rich and strange.
Sea nymphs hourly ring his knell:
Hark, now I hear them. Ding dong bell."

Is it the same bell, I wonder, that can be heard from the cliffs at Dunemoor. The bells from the City beneath the sea. Where it happened. Where I lost my innocence.

Without thinking, I turn down a side street.

# 4

Someone is looking at me.

"Are you OK?" the voice says.

I look up but there is nobody there, just people in the street.

"I won't be long," he had said. Where am I?

I am in a crowd of people, in a rich array of dress. "Folks is folks," Mr Baxter said. We can smile at the unknown, we can shy away from fear, laugh with, in empathy or at, in ignorance, but "folks is folks."

I know no-one and I am no-one. A country girl in the byways of the city. No longer innocent. There, I have said it again. A girl with no faith, yet missing, secretly, in some arcane way, the old cross-sword that she threw away, nothing but false idolatry.

Heresy, burning. Howls of agony in the name of faith. Religion rather, not faith. Surely not God. Underneath we are all naked. Even the figure from the painting was merely a manifestation, yet of energy, divine.

How to draw it down? That is the gift that they all want.

Faith is what I want. Perhaps I should listen to my dreams. Perhaps I should seek the meaning already there.

Look at the devastation in the city, and within, the humanity. The light and dark out of the shadows, one about to take the other out.

I cannot turn away from the path allotted to me, fight it though I would. Yet what has it been to me? Had I not seen the figures of darkness, and lived through the terror of my escape from Burnchester and Shingle Island, and remained haunted by visions of my crying mother's eyes, I would abandon my journey now. Were it not for the thought of the Dark Master who seeks it; the Stranger who wants to take me; Mr Rummage, even the voice of Tom. Like faith in the possibility of something as yet unborn.

I cannot be the only one. And yet, in stories there is always only one hero or heroine. I remember playing out my father's stories, a little bit of magic, or alchemy, thrown in. Curious that the words, like the images, have that transforming power, living in an intermediary space between here and there. Perhaps this story is different.

The "there" of our dreams, and the goal we all know to be true but cannot prove, struggle though we will. We are all the heroines or heroes of our own stories. Perhaps we all carry the cell too.

I look for the boy. I am not alone. Tears fall down my face. He is right. I have to trust. I will trust him. Why have I walked away?

My friend runs out of a shop carrying a bag. A man gives chase.

I run to him, calling, but people get in the way.

The boy stumbles in and out of the crowd.

He crosses the road, looks about him, calls my name. The shopkeeper behind shouts – and now the sound of horns and brakes.

My friend approaches a tube station. I scream at the top of my voice.

A policeman steps out and grabs his shoulder. He hurls him to the ground, punches his knee into his back, then twists the boy's arms and grips his hands.

The boy is in agony.

I rush forward screaming and crying. Another policeman grabs me and holds me back. I struggle. I spit.

It is all over in moments. My friend's struggle is useless. There is fear and rebellion in his eyes. He is young. His eyes smile at mine and then a shadow falls across them.

Other policemen arrive on the scene.

I kick and scream, biting the hand that holds me, drawing blood. I try to reach the prostrate figure on the ground. These are not policemen, that is clear. I try to reach the cell, this time in vain.

They beat the boy badly. I scream and pull as hard as I can. He cannot even cover his head. People protest but the "policemen" threaten them. I break free and fall beside the boy.

The shopkeeper has come up.

"He stole from my shop."

From behind his back, the boy opens his hand and reveals a small packet, which rolls onto the ground. The shopkeeper picks it up.

"You took that. I saw you."

I lift the boy to his feet.

"I saw you," the shopkeeper's anger is dampened by the pain the boy is in, and the beating. He is suspicious. The tiny bag contains nothing but a local map. A trifle in the circumstances.

"Did you take this?" a policeman asks, holding him.

The boy, in deep pain, looks straight at the shopkeeper.

"Do you deny it?"

"What he took was for me," I say, trying to stay calm. "He was doing it for me. I need a map."

I clutch the cell.

I hold my hand out to him.

The boy looks at me, and shakes his head. He looks desperately at the shopkeeper. The policemen are uneasy.

One of them looks me up and down. There is a crackling

over his phone. I allow my arm to drop, and reach the object in my pocket, concentrating hard.

The policeman is about to speak to me, but the the shop-keeper interrupts.

"I do not wish to press charges on this boy. He has received enough punishment already. Let them go."

The man hands me the map. I offer to pay but he shakes his head.

The policeman releases the boy's arm.

"I hope you find what you're looking for," the man says.

I thank the shopkeeper. The boy is free, but he is weakened. I sense that he wants to come with me but something is troubling him.

Perhaps he knows something that I do not. Is he trying to warn me?

"I will need a statement from you two. We can do that in your shop."

The policeman then turns to me.

"Go. Stay out of trouble next time. Especially if it isn't yours."

The boy stares at me, moving his eyes. I stand still but he shakes his head.

I begin to walk away, holding back tears. I look back at him. He nods and mouths something that I cannot make out. Like an instruction. "Meet. I stay on?"

I watch the boy enter the shop with the owner and the policeman. I try to think how to help him. I will wait.

I see a newsagent. The headline reads:

"Parliament threatened."

Some of the security guards, the "policemen", are working for the powers of the dark. I think of the Priory. Of Mr Vespers and Mr Blakemore. Of The Spearhead of Destiny. Of the mysterious secrets of Burnchester, the arcane Chamber, the Stranger, and the haunting figures. Have these figures taken a new shape? I have seen their insignia.

47

I think of the figures standing in line at Burnchester on the fateful night of my escape and of the cries I heard in the fire. "Heresy". "Reformation".

I know that the cell I carry, under the mask of silence and secrecy, under my new disguise, is part of the battle. The possession of which will give victory to the world. I am tempted to destroy it. Yet its power is already clear.

They will take me if they can. I have a little time.

A police car ahead. They are looking for someone.

The car stops. A policeman shows a photograph to a passer-by. The passer-by looks at it and shakes his head. The car moves closer to me.

I head down a side street.

I enter a church. There is an exhibition in the nave.

Someone is serving tea.

I look about me, to check there are no figures here.

I hold my rucsac close to me.

The man at the table, to my relief, serves me without interest. He doesn't want money. He tells me about the paintings. They are his. He tells me to look closely.

Always there are hidden secrets, he says, in everything, everyone. He smiles. He seems strange, but is kind enough.

I walk towards one of the side chapels so that I will not be seen. The pictures spread enchantment about my head. They are very beautiful, I can tell, but I am too distracted and feel overwhelming guilt.

However, as I glance sideways, one painting I do notice. I nearly trip. I put my things down and go over to it.

It is a copy of the painting from the church of St Mary Magdalene.

There it is in detail. Even the surround is there. Including the missing section at the base. Even the surround! With the missing fragment! My heart throbs! I can hardly focus. The artist must have copied it. It is very good. I continue looking.

I cannot read the Latin: "Perge modo et, qua te ducit via...." I get stuck. The tree of many fruit. The Figure. Everything, the Spearhead at the base!

The Spearhead! I nearly choke.

What is it doing here?

I turn to ask the man. I hurry back to the table. I hear chanting.

But there is no-one there. There is not even a table. I am going mad.

I walk back to the painting. The surround has gone. I am in despair.

I go to the entrance door and put my hand in holy water. I spread it on my brow. I don't know why.

I go to the chapel and sit in a pew.

I miss my friend. I get up and go to find a washroom. I try to clean my wound.

I return to the chancel and look at the altar. It is simple. I am lost and bewildered. The past and the present conspiring against me. It was there, the Spearhead. The Instructions. The artist told me to look! As if he knew I was coming!

I put my head into my hands and allow the tears to flow. Gradually, some strength flows back to me through my tears.

I dry my eyes. I look into the altar, now a mirror.

\*

Memories flood back – of the sea, and our boat and the joy that we first felt after we left the harbour at Southwold. I see Jess and Rick and the panting smile of Rompy, my dog, excited by the bustling waves. The journey was all before us. We had instructions and provisions. Jess made sure that we read the instructions, even testing us from time to time.

\*

My attention is drawn by someone entering the church. It is my friend.

I get up as he comes over. I turn to face him, guiltily.

"Here," he says, placing a bag on the table.

"What is it?"

"Take a look."

"I'm sorry I didn't stay. I thought you wanted me to leave."

"You did right. It was better that you left. It's OK."

"What happened?"

"Later," the boy says.

I look at his face. I see his playful, cheeky, eyes. There is a sadness too. I smile. He smiles too.

"Are you alright?"

"They can't hurt me any more."

"I must leave. They are not far behind. It is better that I go alone."

"Why?" The boy asks.

"Tell me your name?" I ask, turning my eyes away.

"I can hide you. My mum could...." he answers.

"I don't have time." I say, checking myself. "They are very close behind. I must leave now."

The boy looks through the open door of the church. On the other side of the road, by the station, two policemen wait. Their heads turn from side to side as the traffic passes.

"I am coming with you," the boy says.

"We must not both be taken again. It is better to remain separate."

"I am not going to leave you."

I do not respond. I put my arms round the boy's neck. I hug him closely.

"Remember to meet, where I said!"

I turn towards the side entrance. I am in the street.

"Hey, wait a minute!" the boy shouts.

I walk fast into the crowds. The boy calls out again, and catches up with me.

"You can't go like that, Tyro. It is you, isn't it?"

I stop. I hold his arm and look at him. I hand him a folded piece of paper.

"Yes."

He looks at me, then at the paper in his hand.

I move too quickly for him. He tries to follow but anxiety makes me swift. I hear the name Jules. Can it be?

I hear him call out, "remember what I said! I am Jules!" I run down a side street.

Tears stream down my face. I am angry at myself.

After a few minutes I pause. I turn back to look for him. I retrace my steps, but he is not there. I cannot find the church. I cannot find him.

I wait, but there is no-one. I cry. I walk on, trying to focus, to remember the things I was supposed to learn.

All that training. What use is it now? I am on my own. I have turned away someone I could love. Nothing else matters. Not even the cell.

I call his name at the top of my voice.

"Jules!"

The name echoes down the streets, as if they were the walls of a hollow cave.

I am in despair.

The city surrounds me.

The stark visions of the country hide in the shadows here, or are more easily concealed. I walk on.

*

A few streets away, an armed policeman watches a car.

Jules, in desperation, goes up to him. He asks if he has seen a girl.

The policeman doesn't answer. His eyes continue to search.

Jules repeats the question.

A girl who was with him? Sure.

51

"Look, son," the policeman says, the barrel of his rifle swinging round, "maybe she's already accounted for. Maybe she wasn't interested! Shouldn't you be in school?"

The policeman looks at him, more closely. Recognises him.

"On the other hand," he says, smartly, "if you can find her for me!"

Jules is angry.

"You're all a bunch of....!"

He runs off, towards the tube.

The policeman shouts down his radio.

*

After the first storm, there came another. So sudden, so ferocious that we hardly had time to speak. We struggled to face the wind and waves. We knew our time had come, our separation imminent. Yet in that moment, or moments rather, we felt closer than we had before. The sadness could not overcome the closeness, the past and present stronger than the future now.

When the wave hit, I remember only one thing that Jess said. "It is Burnchester that has burnt. That was the smoke that stretched across the sky." Even fighting for life she wanted to tell me this and then she told me that we would meet again and that she loved me.

*

In the station, Jules heads for the ticket booth.

"Mr. Did you see a girl?"

The man looks at him.

"Dark eyes. Long hair. Wearing old clothes."

"What are you on? Next!"

The man behind pushes forward.

"Move! I've got a train to catch."

Jules tries to shove him back, then runs for the barrier. Two figures emerge from the shadows and follow. A policeman is watching.

A woman with a suitcase passes through an open gate. Jules scrapes through behind her.

"Hey, you! Stop!" says the guard. "Come back here! Bas....!"

People look round.

The policeman begins pursuit, mouthing instructions into his radio. They have strict rules of engagement, procedures. He releases the catch on the automatic.

Jules runs down the steps, the figures following.

Jules knocks into someone.

There are shouts of "stop that boy!"

People panic. Then they give chase.

Tyro is nowhere to be seen. She must have gone another way. She said she had no money, didn't she?

A policeman – there are others now – shouts for Jules to stop.

There are two ways out: one up the stairs ahead, the other back to the entrance he has just left. He could try the tunnel and hide in one of the recesses along the track. But he might be dead before reaching it. He might be dead anyway.

A man tries to grab him. Jules fights him off. The man smashes him in the face. Jules pulls the man's coat away from him. He turns to run, holding it around him.

Jules leaps up the stairs, taking several steps at a time.

He turns and throws the coat down onto the leading man behind. It lands in his face and the man falls. Others pile on top of him.

There is screaming and shouting.

The police issue a warning. It is no use. The boy has got a lead.

He is close to the top of the stairs by the side exit.

A shot is heard. There is pandemonium. Another man trips and several policemen fall.

A woman, close to the exit barrier, is watching CCTV anxiously.

She sees the boy coming round a corner towards her. She's watched it all. This boy's not a threat. Just got no ticket. What should she do?

Jules looks at the woman, who sees his eyes. They seem wet. He reminds her of her lost son. Died in a street battle. A good boy.

"I haven't been on a train Mrs. I'm looking for someone. A girl. Tyro. Something's happened to her. I must find her. The police.... It's a matter of life or death. You've got to believe me."

The crowd approaches.

"You've got to help me!" Jules points as two figures appear. "I'm going to be killed!"

The woman leans over.

"I'm going to trust you. No girl's passed through this barrier in the last ten minutes. I'll tell them you jumped. Go!"

She opens the barrier, and lets him through.

Jules gives her a kiss and runs into the street. He has not noticed the medallion she wears about her neck.

The monitors hang from the ceiling in front of her. Shots of the boy outside. Another screen shows the figures, the policeman and others about to turn the corner.

"Good luck," she whispers, closing the barrier.

Two policemen run up.

"I could do nothing. Jumped over!"

A policeman shoves her aside and they proceed.

The boy is out of sight.

The figures move on towards the barrier.

"Tyro?" she whispers.

# 5

I am on the High Street. I try to focus.

A woman passes me with a child in a buggy. The child points. The mother looks at me.

I bump into a passer-by who swears angrily.

High above, a helicopter whines.

I cannot stop thinking of Jules. Where is he? What was his father doing at Shingle Island? Why did I leave? I feel more angry and guilty than ever. How bruised he was. How warm.

The latest headline leaps out from a billboard:

"School stand-off continues. Concern over captives grows." A sub-heading reads: "Whereabouts unknown."

I drop a coin into the box and take a paper.

A small piece in the late news column reads: "Mystery at Secret Island. MOD refuses to comment."

Why has it taken so long for this to filter through?

I turn down a side-street and into a square. There is a small Christmas fair on the green.

The map was right. There is a library ahead of me.

Someone is there but the door is locked.

I sit on a bench nearby. I hear the music from the Christmas fair. People loiter near to one of the stalls. A clock strikes nine.

An old man stands close by with his two dogs.

Two shapes beyond him look towards the library.

The music, cheerful in its own way, continues to play. I look at the paper.

The mother and child approach. Three teenagers run past them.

"You lot should be in school!" The mother says.

The child strokes one of the old man's dogs, before coming up to me.

I sense something is wrong. Something is nearby, closing. How far away is it? Is it them?

"You look as if you've seen a ghost," the mother says.

"Do you know where the nearest station is?" I ask.

"On the High Street. It's not far."

The woman looks at me.

"I'll show you, if you like. I'm going shortly."

"Thanks."

The library door opens.

The two shapes have begun to walk in our direction.

"You're that girl, aren't you?" The woman says, as I enter the library.

The librarian glances at the woman and child, the old man and the two figures. She seems to pause.

Inside a notice-board reads:

Reserve Library for The Courtly Institute

*

"Goodgy-goo!" the old man says.

"Ga!" Says the girl.

The two figures have edged closer, their faces hidden.

*

The library reading room is large with a door leading off at the back. There is a staircase in the right-hand corner leading to the floor above, overlooking the square.

To the left is the reception desk, where the librarian is at a computer screen, typing rapidly.

"Good morning," she says, as I make my way to one of the tables.

"Can I help?" she asks.

"I'm OK. Thanks," I reply.

The librarian is in her early thirties. Tall, brown-haired with a strong face, as if carved from an ageless stone. She has a medallion about her neck.

"Is everything OK?" I add, without thinking, without knowing why, as if it had been drawn from me.

The librarian seems momentarily confused, and looks at me.

The screen beside her is divided into sections, one of which shows the news. Another shows camera angles of the entrance and exits to the building, including a side entrance down an alley.

The librarian notices the two figures just outside the door, talking to the lady and the old man.

She types something onto the keypad, looks back at me, then at the door.

She is clearly uneasy.

Various images flash onto one of the screens.

One of them makes the librarian pause. She dials a number. There is a brief, muted conversation, while several more images appear.

I reach the reference section and turn to watch her. She is nervous. There is something familiar about her.

*

Outside, the music has got louder. The dogs are barking. One of the figures shouts at the old man. He has a dark cross-sword etched on to his tunic.

The woman tried to intervene, but she can no longer move. A dark energy has overwhelmed her.

The second figure is at the alley entrance beside the library. A police car has parked in the square. A policeman gets out and hurries over.

*

I am by the map section.

I find one of East Anglia and one of Scotland. I spread them out on a table beside the newspaper which has the photo of mum and Dennis across the front page.

The headline reads: "Secret escape. Fact or fiction? Latest."

I take out the envelope that I keep inside my shirt.

I kiss the photo. I have read the article several times, but cannot believe it to be true. Surely journalists have got this story wrong?

I read it again, in case I have forgotten something.

As I read, I see images of my father. Rick and Jess appear holding on to each other in the storm. I am trying to reach them, but.... there is nothing.

I turn to the maps and open the one of the Northern Highlands.

I see mountains and craggy cliffs and streams and the long coastline. Small roads occasionally cross open country and follow the valleys or parts of the coast, sometimes with great gaps between them, and here there seems to be a black line, which must be the railway. There is a red dot and a name beside it against little more than a house.

This must the station at the far end of the world.

The librarian has put a notice on the door, and locked it. She hurries towards me.

*

Outside mother and child remain paralysed. The old man is still. The dogs next to him.

The figure passes the woman, his head bowed.

"Hey, you! Stop!"

The policeman shouts.

The figure turns and looks into his face. An astonishing energy comes through it, repelling any attempt to counter it, from the dark inset hollow eyes.

At the other side of the park, a third figure watches.

"I'm looking for a girl, officer. Dark eyes. Long hair."

The policeman tries to speak, but in moments, his face is still, as if fixed in stone.

A siren bursts into life.

The third figure moves closer to the library door.

*

"Going on a journey?" the librarian asks, trying to seem calm.

She sees the shape of a mountain range, to which she points.

"I'm trying to find Doonwreath."

"You won't get in there."

"I've got to. It's in these instructions from my Headmaster. I'm also looking for some information about the Spearhead? For my Dad. It's a sort of object. Like the Holy Grail."

"Really?"

"Its proper name is the Spearhead of Destiny. My Dad likes – liked – that sort of thing. He's dead. Mysteries. Nobody knows if it exists. There are lots of stories, even my school.... I've got to go. I'm in a hurry. Please. It's really the Island I'm after. But I'm not sure where it is exactly or how to get there."

"What is your Headmaster's name?"

I hand her Mr Rummage's letter. I notice the librarian's medallion.

She glances at it and hands it back.

"Pick up your things and follow me. And hurry."

I take my things and the maps and follow her to the door at the back.

The long wait has left the librarian a little unprepared but she knows evil is nearby. There is little time.

I know I have been recognised. The shared secrecy is a pact that requires discretion, so I say nothing. There is something soothing in the librarian's voice. As if I recognise it from somewhere.

"We're a long way from the Holy Grail here. Or the Spearhead. Or Doonwreath."

The librarian unlocks a door marked Courtly Institute Reserve, A, and we enter.

I am reminded of the manuscript room at Burnchester. And of the door to the tunnels. The dreams come back to me. Of being trapped; of being followed. Are there tunnels here too?

The librarian tells me to wait, that she'll be back shortly. I look at the old shelves around me, trying to think.

Then I realise. She reminds me of Mr Rummage's colleague, whose mask we found, and who disappeared. She reminds me of Jane Fellows.

*

A police car turns into Park Square, blue light pulsating. Jules follows, out of sight.

The car halts beside the old man, the woman and her daughter, and their colleague. All seem lifeless. They call for an ambulance, then examine the frigid bodies.

They are angry and bewildered. They try to resuscitate them.

*

The librarian hurriedly enters the room, carrying papers, a map and a box.

She hands me one of the papers, and places the rest on the table.

The medallion about her neck gives off a powerful, complex, light. I need to avert my eyes.

"Go to that address. You will be met by a friend of mine. She will have one of these. The energy is unusual, but won't harm you."

The librarian taps the medallion.

"You will be safe. Do what she asks you. Don't be deceived by her humble ways, or if she is secretive. But of others, be careful. The enemy's power is spreading rapidly. We have to move quickly. They are here now."

Before I can ask any questions, she opens the door and leads me out. We turn right, away from the reading room.

\*

The ice-cold waters recede, and are replaced by rocks emerging from the ground. My own fate shudders to the call of Neptune rising.

\*

There is a loud crash from a door behind us. There are screams.

The librarian grabs my arm.

A figure is walking towards us. It is one that followed me to the cafe, and in the street. A policeman holds a rifle close to its back.

"Get out of here!" the policeman shouts to us. "As far away as possible. Go!"

We start to run.

"Stop or I'll shoot!"

The figure ignores him.

The policeman fires but the figure continues to walk.

Then it slows. Blood drips from its wounded back. It turns to reveal the blood soaked cross-sword. The policeman's face is still.

We reach the end of the corridor, and turn out of sight. There is a muffled sound. Then the padding feet begin again.

We are close to the side exit.

"Change into these. Then go."

"I...."

I enter the alcove and throw on the items inside the box. I hurry out into the street.

"Good luck," the librarian calls.

She turns to make her way back.

The figure stands in front of her. Beyond, the policeman lies on the ground, the rifle twisted beside him.

She stares into the thing's eyes. It has no control over one of her order. There are only three of which it is afraid, and this is one, more ancient than itself. Nevertheless, it will fight.

The figure raises its hands, but its energy is low.

"How dare you! We will follow her to the ends of the earth, wherever she goes. We will destroy her! And take what is ours!"

The librarian studies its bony hand.

The figure tries to move forward but cannot.

"What do you want from me?" It asks.

"You cannot take what is not allotted."

The figure draws up to its full height and swipes its foul bloodied hand across the librarian's face. She falls to the ground.

"We will!"

The librarian gets up. The medallion's powerful light, forces the figure to avert its eyes.

"So it is war. You have chosen."

She stands her ground. The foul-stenched figure remains still. It cannot move past her.

"Time will soon be ours! We will destroy you!"

She turns to the exit that Tyro took, opens it, and follows. She senses the figure behind her, but it cannot touch her.

She hopes that the earthly help that she has summoned, is not too late.

*

At the front of library, ambulance staff carry the human figures into their vehicles.

There are several police cars now. Soldiers await in the background. HQ has been alerted. So has the Prime Minister's office. This is the first definite manifestation since Burnchester and, if what they believe is right, Shingle Island. The enemy has reached London.

Inside, several armed police stand guard. Two others carry their wounded comrade from the corridor.

Another armed group have gone down the side alley.

"You think it's them?" one of them asks.

"Looks like it. Let's hope there are only two of them. If there are more, we're in real trouble."

"We're in trouble anyway."

The officer takes a call.

"There has been a major security alert around Parliament."

*

Jules reaches the back exit as a young woman leaves.

"Excuse me!" he calls, but she hurries on.

Behind them, the second figure has appeared. Armed police follow.

Jules runs up to the woman who turns. She sees the figure.

There is a momentary movement in her eyes, as if in warning.

"Tyro?"

She walks on, tears in her eyes.

Why doesn't she respond?

The alley seems endless. There are shadows on either side, recesses, hidden entrances, detritus.

The police, behind the figure, have seen the two young people beyond, and must be cautious. But they cannot let this prize go.

"Stop! Or I'll shoot!" one of them bellows, "Hands up! High!"

The figure ignores him. They run towards it.

The policeman screams a second warning.

I start to run, calling Jules.

More shouts. I weave sideways, and hold out my hand. Jules takes it.

The loud crackle of gunfire.

The bullets lodge in the back of the figure, who stumbles, but does not fall.

I turn to see its face. It seems the same that followed me before. It is undaunted by the wound.

In his hand it carries an object. A small broken cross. The one that I threw away. It is the Stranger.

"What do you want?" I cry. "Go back to the evil place where you reside!"

Jules is beside me.

"Give yourself up. Give the object up. Or...." he breathes.

I will not be cowed.

"You will be destroyed. Give me the object!"

"Never!" I cry defiantly.

I look at Jules, and turn.

Two policemen tackle the Stranger to the ground, its feet sliding in a line of its own blood.

The cross falls and slides forward. It is now or never. Jules runs forward and picks it up.

"Tyro! Tyro!" He calls, as I run on.

A policeman shouts for help.

I turn and look at Jules.

"Tyro?"

My eyes reveal all.

"Tyro! It's you isn't it? I told you, I'm coming with you."

The policeman calls again. Jules turns and goes to help.

I shout at him to follow, but he does not hear. I dare not wait.

Jules holds back tears as he helps the policeman to his feet. He still has my old cross in his hand. The figure and the other policeman lie beside him on the ground.

"Thanks," the policeman says.

Jules reaches the alley exit.

Several police cars screech to a halt.

Police spill out all ways; two run to their colleague; three try to hold the Stranger on the ground.

His strength is astonishing. It is only with the use of the policemen's high voltage weapons that he is stalled.

Jules is stopped.

"Wrong way, son! You're not going anywhere."

Jules struggles free.

The second figure joins the Stranger. They throw the policemen off, and continue their steady steps.

A second woman disappears into the crowd, followed by Jules.

The police shout another warning to the figures, then to the crowds to disperse.

There is panic. People try to protect the women and children, others flee. There is screaming. People are terrified.

There is a crackling of gunfire.

Several people are wounded. More police arrive.

Tyro, the librarian and Jules are out of sight.

The figures dissolve into the crowd.

There is pandemonium.

*

As I hurry on, my energy begins to return, though my guilt increases. The cross-sword, picked up by Jules, confirms that the Stranger and his crew have come from Burnchester. It gives me added hope, a companion to the cell. Yet it frightens me too.

I know that even if it worked once, it won't again. It brings memories, but its time is passed.

Only a new image will help to draw down and activate the energy for the pursuit of the goal, for the pursuit of my journey. Yet it was born of the old.

I must become my own image maker, though I do not know enough of the source of its magic and its art. Perhaps with the aid of the cell?

I want to bring forth images into the light and let them grow. But the cell represents something more, otherwise enemies would not want to possess it. Perhaps it has something of the darkness in it too.

A helicopter throbs overhead.

*

I reach a street and wait.

My heart stirs for the people around me, as I look out for Jules. I want to share their journeys. But my heart must carve its own path in their image.

On the walls are graffiti: against war, poverty, madness. A politician's smile of eternal optimism, of inevitable deceit. The sickness of power.

Jumbled letters are painted by a church gate. The very same that I saw in the Domed Chamber: muchbuhijushin

*

A bus reaches the lights beside me as they turn red. In desperation, I jump on.

The top is empty. I check the address that the librarian gave me. I check the object. Will it work again? I watch the streets. I look for Jules. Perhaps I am better alone.

The bus stops in front of a railway bridge.

There are voices below. My body freezes.

The shouting gets louder. Footsteps can be heard on the stairs.

I see people reflected in the window. Policemen and.... yes.... Jules!

His eyes are trying to tell me something. He glances at the police. He holds the cross-sword in his hand. I look at the window and he nods.

I focus all my energy.

I lift my foot and drive it through the pane. Glass falls everywhere as I clamber out.

The policemen try to follow but Jules blocks their path.

As I exit, Jules scrambles back over the seats and runs down the stairs.

I stretch my arms above the bus to the face of the bridge. Reaching some lateral wires, I heave myself onto the wall. There is a station to my left.

I hear the rumble of an arriving train and hurry to get on.

The doors begin to close as Jules, who has run up the stairs, forces himself on.

Two policemen run alongside as the train pulls away. One rages down his phone.

They run down the stairs into a waiting car.

I sit anxiously, confused.

People stare into the aisle, others read.

I try to think of the safe house, but cannot. I want to be with Jules, but I think I'm better alone.

Jules comes through a dividing door, looking from side to side. I lower my head. I will stick to my plan, despite my aching heart. Jules has seen me. I smile.

The train slows. Embankment station. The doors open.

Passengers exit. I make for a door, hold back behind a passenger. Jules loses sight of me. As the doors close he turns to the place where I was sitting.

At that moment, I step out onto the platform.

I watch his face staring at me from behind the window. He tries to wrench the door open. I try from the outside. It is too late.

The train moves forwards, and I run along beside it. There is a longing in his eyes.

Jules mouths one word: "Why?"

I feel tears welling up.

The train enters the tunnel.

I turn towards the exit.

I should not have doubted. How will I find him again?

*

"Tickets! All tickets!"

I have neither ticket nor money to buy one. There are the policemen again, beyond by the barrier.

A woman wearing dark glasses, knocks into me. She holds a thin white stick ahead of her.

"Tickets please! Move along there!"

The CCTV cameras whir. I breathe in and try to steady. As the passengers approach the barrier, I whisper into the woman's ear, taking her arm.

"Have your tickets ready."

The ticket collector takes each one. One by one people file through. The blind woman is next. The collector takes the ticket from the younger woman at her side, and allows them through.

Outside the station, the blind woman allows herself to be accompanied a little further, past the police cars, to a waiting bus.

The blind woman thanks me. Then takes off her glasses and

puts them in her pocket. She folds the stick and puts it into her bag. I notice a second woman by the bus, with a dog on a lead.

She comes over to us. The "blind" woman looks at me. It is none other than the librarian. Her medallion sparkles. Her friend's dog is pulling hard, and whimpering.

It is dear old Rompy.

He is all over me, leaping and barking and licking and jumping. He runs round and round. I cannot believe it. He cannot either.

I thank the lady who brought him. I thank the librarian. I want to know who the lady is and how she found Rompy, but there is no time for explanations, as the police are watching. They whisper "good luck" and walk hurriedly away.

I pat Rompy's head, and begin to cry.

# 6

I love Rompy, but am fearful as I walk into the West
End. I have lost Jules and the figures will not be long
behind.

I pace along the Embankment with Rompy, my mind in full
flow. Who was the librarian? How did she know so much
about me? Was she Jane Fellows? Who was the other lady?
I will find Jules.

The river is close to the top of the wall. Army units place
sandbags along it. The Houses of Parliament are ahead.

A police tannoy warns of more flooding.

People walk hurriedly towards the station, wait at bus
stops. Evacuation has begun.

Across the river, in the winter light, is The National
Theatre. The words "Shakespeare's Company" in bright red.

To the east and west, bridges link north and south.

The grey band of tide shifts and dances. Boats parry the
moving water, driftwood bobs like seals.

\*

I reach Trafalgar Square. I recognise, from childhood, the
National Gallery, St Martin-in-the-Fields. Our last visit was
just before my father died.

I see him standing at the base of Nelson's column. A

photographer is taking a picture of me with a parrot on my shoulder. My mother next to me.

Rompy and I cross the road. He has undying enthusiasm.

People move in a slow dance: on the lions, beside the fountain. Others look at maps, take photos of the snow.

A Christmas tree guards the centre. Decorations brighten buildings. Carols reach us from the church.

Cars, queues. Pigeons feeding in the dusk.

More police. On alert.

Along Whitehall, everywhere cameras, lest we forget that privacy is dead.

Police buses, military vehicles. They have received intelligence. Heard the news. There is something darker. The virus spreads.

I sense something hidden.

We are being invaded by darker energies, beneath the shouts, the laughter. Close-by.

*

The evening sky is darkened by towers over Admiralty Arch.

I look for the shapes I saw at sea.

I wonder where the separation lies between the dark within and the gathering storm.

Some of the figures who invaded Burnchester were figments of the collective mind, yet some were not. Keep watch and ward, for that is the perilous delusion that the Dark Master seeks to create, so leading us into temptation, against the wrong enemy, who is but a decoy and a fiction against the real dark, which is the darkness of ignorance and of pride, and blind ambition, and a will to power.

I recall the blank mask in Mr Baxter's lessons. How its visage filled with fears brought forth by the enactment of the witches' scene. I will test my ability to imprint onto others, that which is hidden in me, and test what happens when I draw the projection back and look at the person as a unique being needing love.

*

A group of schoolchildren pass. One whispers. Another skips, more urge her on. There is laughter. The teacher frowns. The children have no shadows – yet.

Whitehall is famed throughout the world for its symbolism, its theatricality, being more than a gesture of history.

Concrete slabs, like giant's teeth front a long building. Soldiers with rifles. The Ministry of Defence lies like a powerless, injured king.

An old Volvo is parked. It seems familiar. I must be dreaming! I scribble a note, and put it under the wiper.

Reports from Burnchester lie on a desk, beside incidents from other countries, from colleagues in the field.

The summer de-briefings return to me. Past and present fuse into a moment of precognition.

The threat is global, and its face obscure, like the King of the Underworld's mask of invisibility, stalking every nation upon earth.

I am being filmed. Who is this, outside our gates? What does she carry? Is she a threat?

Shall I tell them what I have seen? No. Only the Prime Minister.

Along the river the enemy moves stealthily forwards. The figures climb over the embankment walls.

I hurry on.

An empty bus rumbles to a stop, like Hope's pallbearer. People lurch forward.

The horses snort from across the road. Rompy is alert. I think of the sacrifices that Jules has made. I think of the sacrifices that many have made.

Along the East Anglian coast, barrels cast off their toxic spells. Out of them, figures rise and begin their march.

*

Massive security. Downing Street.

*

Cobra. Where are the people from Burnchester? What happened at Shingle Island? What to do about the imminent threat?

Secondary causes take prime position in the political landscape.

Can Mr Rummage's secret plan be salvaged? Without it we are doomed! Except that the politicians know nothing of it. It is above top secret. The intelligence service knows the limits of the political elite. Mr Rummage is a clever man.

*

I will return, and find a way in.

I am by the river next to the Houses of Parliament. Waves motion in serpents' coils.

I am on Westminster Bridge. "I know of no politics in the cause of human happiness." The inimitable said so himself. Big Ben, like a sentinel, beats a crescent tune along with time, and to its right, the Great Abbey Church of St Peter. Ding Dong Merrily On High.

Unseen, behind Parliament, figures line the shadows.

Others move towards the Abbey Church. Yet more, filter into the streets of state. There are no sensors clever enough to tell.

Inside, the House is in uproar.

The Prime Minister has finished a speech.

Members of Her Majesty's Government cry, "Hear! Hear!"

Members of the opposition cry "Shame! When will the Prime Minister tell us the truth?"

Mr Speaker cries.

"Order! Order!"

"It's lies! The truth! The truth"

"Order! I say!"

Mr Speaker raises his hands.

"Order! Order!"

The noise grows.

A huge cheer.

The Honourable Member who cried "lies" is led out.

Howls from the opposition. Another roar.

"The leader of the opposition, The Honourable Member for...."

The lobby journalists lean forward. The Prime Minister's fate is in the balance. Like the security of the State. Perhaps of the world.

*

Outside a police marksman looks down from the roof in horror. The water has breached the wall. He picks up his phone. He does not see the figures.

*

"The Prime Minister has failed the House and the people of this country.

He has failed to protect the State from a deadly enemy. The

situation is one of immense gravity. He has failed to inform or to act."

Excitement has given way to fear.

"In fact, he has failed in every respect. Our defences are in turmoil. The fabric of the nation is crumbling. The Prime Minister has therefore forfeited his right to govern. I call upon the Prime Minister to resign. Before it is too late! To resign now!"

*

Outside, the winter crows shift on their perches, like dark angels waiting for prey as yet to be exhumed.

*

The Prime Minister stands. Looks about him. He must draw forth all available energies, especially the darkest.

Never before has he been required to reach such depths of artifice, cover so skilfully the solitude of his ignorance, project so magnificently the strength of his conviction.

Never has he had the opportunity to be more dominant, or been more desirous of victory.

Or been more vulnerable.

"The Leader of the Opposition knows that the government is doing everything in its power to ensure the safety of all its people. It does not, however, want to create panic...."

The House erupts. The Leader of the Opposition is on his feet.

"Does not the Prime Minister see that by refusing to give any details of the catastrophe at Shingle Island – a key strategic site – more panic, not less, will ensue?

That unless information is forthcoming as to the nature of the threat, and what he is doing about it, people will take to the streets. In fact they are doing so already!"

"We do not have the specific information to make that assurance! As to the rest, we cannot disclose details."

"So the threat is not real?"

Total uproar.

"Our intelligence services have assured us that the threat is there. It has never been government policy (of any party) – to reveal such details. There is a genuine and real threat, though it is not as yet specific. And we do not know who is behind it."

"Burnchester surrounded. Hundreds of adults, hundreds of children missing, possibly deceased. Shingle Island out of contact. Infiltration growing. Communication systems broken. Reports of a major attack in East London. Parliament threatened. Not specific?"

"Order, order!"

"Our intelligence services tell us that it could constitute a major threat to the long term stability of the State. But it is not in the usual category! We will make a full announcement in due course!"

"Could? Due course?" "Long term!"

A phrase, along with trust and information, not normally in the domain of the political elite.

"Usual?"

"Category?"

The Prime Minister sits.

He knows that the opposition knows that they have no solution either. They have to fight together or they are doomed.

"I repeat! The Prime Minister has lost the confidence of the House, and of the people. It is time for him to go, and go now!"

A lobby correspondent hurries out. His name is Veech.

*

In front of Parliament, I feel the growing dark energy. An emerging secret power.

The gates open. Armed guards keep a demonstration back.
The Prime Minister's car leaves first.

A man is watching me from the press entrance.

I walk towards the Great Abbey Church. Will it survive another thousand years?

The heartbeat of a nation is supplied by martyrs' blood.

Someone is carried out of the great West Door. A priest is at the door. Policemen stand by. The ambulance moves away.

People are in a state of shock, some crying.

A newspaper seller shouts the latest news.

The man comes over.

"That wasn't an accident you know," he says.

The ambulance is at the lights in front of us.

I look through the window. The victim's face is obscured.

The lights turn green.

"I'm glad I've found you. You're...," the man lowers his voice, "Tyro, aren't you?"

My heart misses a beat.

The ambulance speeds away. A face stares at me through the window. Its anguished mouth tries to spell something, but I do not understand. The face is pulled back, forced down. It is a face that I know.

"Parliament is surrounded. Head north immediately. There is very little time."

The man is clearly agitated.

"I have something for you."

He looks about him, then takes an envelope from his pocket and hands it to me.

"A press pass into Downing Street. An invitation. I repeat. The enemy are here. Follow your path. Trust no-one. No-where is safe. The last train north leaves at nine. Be on it."

"Who are you?"

"This is also for you."

He hands me a small parcel.

I look at it.

"Who is it from?"

"Someone in the pay of the God of the crossroads."

I look into the man's face. I think I recognise him.

An angry crowd has gathered outside the Great Church. There is an altercation, police come up.

One is watching us.

"Are you? You're.... Mr.... Veech? Mr Veech! Is it you? Why the secrecy? I've been trying to find you. Oh, thank you. Thank you. What news from Burnchester? My mother, Mr Rummage? How did you get out? How did you find me? Tell me!"

"Later. I'll come to the station. If I'm not taken. I have important information. Observe the Prime Minister. In that...."

He points to the parcel.

"Make sure it gets to Mr Rummage. I must go."

The policeman is closing in on us. I shudder. Two figures are looking in our direction. Mr Veech is shaking.

"Are you alright? Mr Veech?"

"Remember, Tyro. I was there. And good luck."

He is about to say more, but he hurries away.

I call after him, "Thank you. I will remember what you said. How can I reach you?"

His shape is fading. He turns, and waves gently. I recognise him more easily now, as we used to see him at Burnchester. I need to know more. I start to follow but a voice stops me.

"Having trouble, luv?"

The policeman catches my shoulder.

"Get off!" I say angrily.

I do not want to be taken for questioning.

"What happened in the church?" I ask.

"Someone got injured."

"Badly?"

"A piece of masonry fell. Unusual. Unprecedented, even. A stone decided it had had enough. Perhaps it was pushed. It's not any church, is it? All the Kings and Queens of England are married and buried here."

"I have to go."

"A word of warning. You should be careful who you speak to. These are dangerous times. Darkness spreading."

I begin to leave.

"There's going to be a lot more trouble. I should get away from here. Some say we're being taken over."

An old Volvo passes by. Inside is my uncle. Uncle Dennis! So it's true. They have escaped! I cannot believe it. The car is way down Victoria Street.

"I'll take your advice, officer."

I walk away, following the alley Mr Veech took. I call his name. I think of Dennis. If he has escaped.... Should I have followed?

I reach the Sanctuary Square. Why would a stone fall? I recall the face in the ambulance.

I cross the square.

I reach the streets behind, opaque, unvisited.

Why did Mr Veech not identify himself? Why was the policeman watching him?

I walk through a cobbled yard, along a gaslit alleyway, through a guarded gate, into a shaded street.

I know that the instruments of darkness are nearby.

Above me the great Abbey rises: faith, image, power. Where crystal light flickers on the altar, and poets lie enchanted by the eternity of their words.

Ahead is an ambulance. Two men attending another on the ground.

I see the face of the dead man. Mr Veech. Two incisions to the neck. I fall and weep. I go over to the men but they push me aside. They carry the body into the vehicle and drive away.

I reach Bickton Street, in tears, barely able to walk.

Sirens echo beyond the medieval walls. The winter leaves lie broken on the ground.

Big Ben strikes.

An armed policeman guards one of the houses.

I walk up to it and ring.

I pass through the side gate watched by the guard.

A car carrying Dr Bartok pulls up two doors down. A man holds a gun to his back.

*

In a discreet square nearby, Church leaders are in session.

The murder of the Bishop remains a profound concern, though he is becoming a martyr. The finger points to the Priory. The discovery of the parchment at Burnchester, details of which have filtered out, must be faced.

The possible discovery of the Spearhead could be beneficial. The confirmation of the tomb in France, would not. Simpler to suppress both. To this end the Churches are united.

However, there is more. The "loss" of the painting at the Church of St Mary Magdalene, has been followed by the falling of the huge cross from the roof of the nearby catholic cathedral, causing panic amongst worshippers. The image on it has been wiped clean. The huge cross hangs suspended by its arms, with the base embedded in the aisle. Vandals, enemies of the church, are being blamed.

Sacred images behind the altar of the Abbey Church have been erased. Nobody knows how or why. Nobody knows how the roof stone fell. The enemies of the church are numerous, but this seems to be the work of the devil.

# 7

We are in a medieval hall.

At one end is a raised dais, on which stands a long altar-like table, with a silver cross at its centre.

A woman stands at a podium on the dais. She wears the habit of a deaconess. The atmosphere is sombre.

The sound of the choir can be heard in the background.

Most of the audience are in clerical clothes, some richly coloured, including Archbishops and Bishops.

"Fellow brothers and sisters, I suggest that we have no choice but to say publicly it was a heart attack. If we acknowledge the truth, we will draw unhelpful attention to ourselves. For the moment, we should allow the investigation to continue out of the glare of publicity. Either way, the Bishop has become a martyr, something we should not forget in the coming months."

The priestess sits down. It is not many years ago that there could not have been a woman to speak in these robes. It is not many more, before the highest office in the church will be a woman's also. Perhaps the Roman brethren are envious.

*

"In the beginning, God created the heaven and the earth...." Alternatively, the feminine principle self-germinated out of chaos.

*

Several people indicate that they wish to speak. The chairperson, who sits behind the cross at the centre, calls for one of them.

A male cleric stands.

"And privately, brothers and sisters? Are we so afraid to speak the truth amongst ourselves for fear of upsetting our Catholic friends?"

"May I remind you that we have a special representative from Rome present, in addition to our usual colleagues."

"The Almighty, I feel sure, would not wish us to hide the truth, though perhaps our Catholic colleagues need another authority to guide them, even interpret it. Their Master is, of course, a great and humble man."

One of the Catholic observers is about to object, but a fellow priest pulls him back.

They have been used to persecution, as they have been used to persecuting, and the cycle of influence, as they read it, is moving in their direction again, so perhaps they are in a strong position. Besides, it is better to hear what they might be accused of – though they know already – than to suffer the deceits of innuendo.

It may or may not be that they already know the identity of the Bishop's killer.

The tentacles of faith are like the roots of a tree, widespread, with one aim only, to sustain the power above, from below.

Yet they are more troubled than they show, for the Priory continues to – how shall we put it – influence them.

The race to confirm the evidence is running its course; for which reason they await news from France.

"I think we all know that I am referring to the suggestion that the Bishop was murdered. Murdered by a group for a document which would destroy us all. A group historically connected to Rome."

The Catholic priest rises.

"I cannot let that pass! Are you suggesting that our Holy Church has any connection whatsoever to the group you say – I remind you there is no evidence – is being suspected for the Bishop's death?"

The first speaker does not respond. He looks around the room, as if to gauge the audience reaction, and then fixes his gaze on the cross.

"On behalf of my own Archbishop (the priest turns and bows) and the Holy Father, and our Holy Roman church, I demand an unequivocal retraction!"

The chairperson does not intervene.

"If my Roman colleague will give his guarantee that the so-called Priory and his own representatives have not had a recent meeting, I shall be pleased to retract."

"I...." but the priest is again pulled back. He bends his head to listen to his Archbishop's advisor. He speaks again.

"The suggestion is scandalous!"

He draws in breath.

"It must be evident that even if there was a meeting – and I do not confirm that there was – that is not the same thing as sanctioning murder. The suggestion is outrageous, unworthy of anyone in Holy Office."

The ambiguity in the priest's response is, for some, not so far from being an admission, though others are unhappy at the Inference – for a scandal in one tradition is not always of benefit in another. Nevertheless, there remains a suspicion, and like a seed, it only awaits the right conditions to flower.

The first speaker, sensing the mood of his audience, responds. His own Archbishop looks on. There is general disquiet on both sides.

"This is not the time for doctrinal debate, nor for airing ancient historical disputes.

We face a common enemy – whose power has been greatly increased by the acquisition of the parchment. I do not need to stress how dangerous its implications are. The whole Church, of whatever tradition, is under threat. Many people already believe, what the Priory will now only apparently confirm. We must unite in defeating it. I suggest therefore a truce, and more open co-operation. There is also the matter of The Spearhead, which it seems, has gone missing."

"Missing?"

*

Inside the house, I am greeted by a lady.

She has a medallion about her neck. I sense she is disguised.

"I'm glad you came. Your old Headmaster would be pleased."

"Mr Rummage? Has he escaped?"

"I have no news. He issued instructions some days ago. We have been watching you since you left Burnchester. The plan will be more difficult without him, but we must try."

"We?"

The lady leads me down a corridor, after leaving Rompy on guard.

"Instructions?"

"To take soundings of...."

"What?"

"Your mind. If Mr Rummage is right – and with Dr Bartok's expertise – we hope to find clues that will help us. Clues for the journey."

"Everyone has a mind.... Why me?"

"Not everybody has glimpsed the Spearhead. And what might come next. By the way, we know about your friend."

"Jules? Where is he? Where can I find him?"

"Later. For the moment, we must enter where neither you – except occasionally in dreams – nor anyone, has seen."

I feel as if I am being invaded.

"The point is that your unconscious, we believe, may reveal images that will be invaluable. I.... We have watched you from an early age. You have heard of the Dream Notation Chamber?"

"Dr Bartok used it for Mrs Limpet and Mr Gruff."

"This is for a more positive reason. We hope to see a glimpse of the language of the future. That might help release the energy. Even lead to a future Grail."

*

Dr Bartok and his guard reach the bottom of a dark, spiral stair. They come to a wall where occasional windows look into a vast, domed room. One is open.

Dr Bartok climbs through and places a recording disc into a machine by the chair. Before returning he checks that his guard is not watching. He makes an adjustment, then climbs back out. And waits.

*

"However, there is a risk."

"A risk?"

"The powers of darkness need the information too, if they are to succeed in their ambition."

"Which is?"

"To rule forever. They know a little of Mr Rummage and your father's dream, but not yet the detail, only the goal. They will destroy it if they can, and our futures with it."

"My....?"

The lady puts a finger to her lips.

We enter a lift and descend.

The door opens onto an area of white marble, about which are several doors. One is marked, BH. Another DNC.

We enter the latter. It is a large circular room with a domed roof. Like the Domed Chamber at Burnchester.

In the centre – where the plinth at Burnchester would have been – is a chair, surrounded by instruments of various kinds.

There are screens showing places that I do not recognise, some in other parts of the world, others of what seems deep space.

On the wall are twelve windows. One of them is open.

The lady asks me to sit, assuring me that we will not be long. All I have to do is relax and allow my mind the freedom to roam.

She will record my brain activity. This will provide an electronic record of the images that are present and latent in my imagination – the first of which will be projected onto the dome roof. The second, which reside in the nether regions of my mind, we will not see, but can be later examined. Here the greatest clues are likely to be. My body sensor network will also be monitored.

What clues do they hope to find? What can my father and Mr Rummage's dream be?

The recording systems are activated. I begin to relax.

At first, the dome is white, which reminds me of the empty frame in the Church of St Mary Magdalene. Then it darkens.

I fear that my mind will show nothing. That I am not the person everyone thinks I am. I try to think of the material that cannot be seen. Like dormant images. How can they be recorded? What did she mean by "language of the future, that might help release the energy, even lead to a future Grail?"

I try to recall the conversations between Dr Bartok, uncle Dennis and Mr Rummage. But I remember nothing.

I hear the rush of a wind, as if from space. Then a chant, which seems to enter through the one open window, like a low murmur, deep underground. Its energy is dark and subtle. Like a captive giant in pain.

The chanting grows and the dark encompasses me. My consciousness begins to fade.

*

In my imagination, I see into space. Constellations move subtly, aeons and aeons of light and time. These are replicated and projected onto the dome. What is happening in my unconscious I cannot know.

Somewhere there our future lies, the place visible for those who can see.

I see dynamic patterns at every stage of growth, from birth to death and resurrection.

I imagine places of great strangeness that only another mind could draw forth. Whose mind?

I think of my own task: to find the place to plant the cell. How?

"Hidden Universe: Secret Power". Is it there, where the cell must lie? What kind of a place is that?

I sense enormous power beneath the earth.

*

Outside the sky is dark, like a closed curtain over the city. The guard and Dr Bartok wait.

*

"What are these images?" I ask, as if in a dream.

"If only we knew the language! We have yet to unravel the emerging signs. Your journey, our journey, depends upon it."

"How is that to be done?"

"Secret knowledge, lost knowledge. Wisdom accumulated over the ages, scattered and hidden within closed groups. Among it, the manuscripts you have seen."

87

"The Priory? The Order of the Magdalene?"

My companion says nothing.

"Will I travel alone, on my journey?"

"No. Some have already begun theirs. Not the same road, but the same destination. It may be some time before you meet."

"Who are they? My mother has gone, my father has gone, my best friends have gone. I am afraid of getting close to the one I might now love. It is as if my solitude protects me from pain."

"Because you have suffered in the past, does not mean you will always suffer. Besides, there are many who suffer more. Never forget that.

You must lose something more, in order to love. Life is a series of changes, deaths. Each is a stepping stone to something higher. God, or whatever principle you believe in, needs recognition, for him or her to complete their work, just as you need God or the principle, to discover your path, and recognise others'."

"And if I don't believe?"

The lady's hand seems to tighten.

"In Him and Her? If I have no principles?" I ask.

"Where is the object?" The lady asks.

Perhaps I should give it up, and abandon my journey. But the figure from the painting made me swear. The figure that came down from the picture and left an empty frame. The figure-image that had life. A life to come.

*

I close my eyes. Out of the darkness, the palest light spreads over the dome above.

From the depth of furthest space I hear a low tone, like a pulse.

The figure from the painting was nothing but an image.

88

Can I have made a pact with an image? Yet it seemed real. Somewhere between the canvas and me, we seemed to meet. The image has gone and the space is now blank. What would happen if all the frames in all the churches and galleries became blank? As if the blood had drained from the images that endorse belief, or wonder.

Above me, I see a rootless tree. Pure white, bordered by time, looking onto eternity. We are all looking into it. Hoping for a sign. A glimpse of.... and then the tree takes root, and grows, and the roots deepen and spread and the tree expands into the light and its leaves become golden, and it is covered with fruit of many kinds. The fruits ripen and fall, in the sunset of the first cycle, and from the seeds, others begin to grow with a re-emerging sun. Just like the image in the surround of the painting, where the Spearhead fell, from the blood from which the tree grew. But here there is no blood. Only the roots of the tree and the leaves and the fruit spreading upward, like an eagle looking at the sky.

I feel spirits entering the image. I go beyond the image, higher and higher, far above the domed room, flying on free wings above London, then so high that I see the whole of the country, and way to my right, the subtle haven that was once Burnchester.

I cross swiftly to it, and gaze beneath the earth into the Domed Chamber. Then I guide my vision through the doors of the Church of Mary Magdalene, and face the empty frame.

I search the surround for the information that I need.

But a voice, awaking from the depths of my past, breaks through.

I panic. I am being watched. There is treachery as there was at Burnchester. If I see what I need to know, others will take it and use it for their ends. The incantation grows. The enemy is present.

I return to the Dome where the obelisk stands, and in a flash, I see the Spearhead. Then it is gone.

*

I am in the chair, eyes open. Whatever power I host is not mine to control.

I imagine other images as yet unformed, emerging into the new symbols of my destiny.

But at whose bidding, under whose hand? Whose control? And why?

Are these the unformed images from below?

The Image Maker is the prince of thought and belief, drawing forth what is latent both here and there, into the middle ground.

Is she the Princess too?

I turn to my companion.

Who is she? She seems to understand my thoughts.

I follow her eyes upwards. She has been sent to help me.

"Where is the object?" She asks.

The pulse from deep space turns into a low melody, like waves of light beamed out of oblivion. As if something is trying to communicate, from somewhere beyond time. From the beginning.

The lady listens. It may be a sign. Her face lights up. I answer, unwillingly.

"Attached to a belt in the small of my back."

"It has drawn the enemy, who will stop at nothing for their darker purpose.

Yet it can also hide when it chooses. You will not have complete control over it. But respect it and do what you can."

How does the lady know about the object's properties? It is as if she has understood something not foretold.

"What do the enemy know?"

"They know that the object has great power, but they do not know its true purpose. That is why they might misuse it, especially without others' knowledge, including your own.

Nor are they certain if they can take the object from you. So they seek both. If they do not achieve their aims, they...."

"Will destroy me. Thanks!"

I want to leave. I want to run. I have nowhere to go. The DNC is doing its job. What of the hidden part? I will hold something back. Until I am ready and the world is ready. How arrogant I have become.

The machines continue to record.

"I hate the object. I hate the journey. I hate myself."

The dome goes blank like a shroud.

The chanting reaches a crescendo. The enemy walks. The walls shake. The music grows.

*

I feel as empty as on the day that my father died.

I didn't believe it at first. I tried to pretend that it hadn't happened, but my mother's tears, and the agony of the months that followed, were proof. My mother and I, in our own way, had died too.

Then, slowly, slowly, with the emerging spring I calmed, and through summer my mother became herself again, at least as near herself as was possible. And what did she do with the love that she lost? Gave it to me.

And I went into myself, and pretended to be happy, until I believed it. I continued to play until the day of our return to school at Burnchester, when memories of my father came back to haunt me, and the old trouble began again.

That's when I started the painting that I have on my wall at home. The one with red in my hair, and blood on my face, looking out onto a distant sunset.

I feel for the object. The music is clear.

Out of the darkness I hear a voice.

"How can you love your neighbour if you hate yourself?"

I turn towards the lady.

How does she know what the enemy knows? I seem to see in her face, two faces. One like a dark shape, the other her own. And behind both, the Dark Master watches like an Angel of Death. Watched by the Angel of Heaven.

Are the faces mine too?

Dark figures cross an ancient landscape.

They seem to come from shadows behind a mountain, out of the caves of the sloping hills, out of the forest trees, from the rocks themselves, an army of silent figures between me and the mountain, waiting, as if to trap me when I journey forward.

I step towards them, unafraid. The mountain folds into mist. I enter a forest.

The figures are the whispers of the trees.

I hear singing and chanting along the path, or a parallel path to mine.

I reach a tree whose roots bridge the path, like serpents sleeping. Above sits an owl, the moon behind. The bird looks as if I were not there and disappears into the leaves. I lie at the base of the tree and fall asleep.

Above me the skies are turbulent. I hear the cries of the gathering storm.

Yet within these cries the clearest tones emerge, as if to guide me.

The enemy is here. Within.

I see the open window in the wall.

I sit up, confused.

There is someone there!

My companion helps me to stand. My clothes conceal the belt, which I try to untie.

I am drained, but I have recorded the melody in my mind. I must find the Lord of the Dance.

I glance again through the window in the wall. I see a face, then another, and they are gone.

I turn away, bewildered by the thought of my discovery – that she has seen them too.

I rage at the deception, but I cannot bring myself to question her.

I throw the belt into the air.

It reels like a snake in water, the central pouch like an eye.

It lifts higher and higher, before breaking into the night air of London, and takes its place amidst the surrounding stars. The eye, like a new planet, looks down, commanding me to follow.

It becomes detached from the belt and now seems to come from a distant galaxy, part of a constellation whose shape I recognise, far, far from the earth. Whose identity the enemy seeks.

It is this now – star that is calling me. But its light is intermittent. The energy insufficient.

The pulse is half rehearsed, and I only half ready to proceed/succeed. The music is the other language that I must unravel.

The eye planet fades.

The night sky returns to its old self. Something falls from where it hung, like a seed from a cradle. Perhaps a single cell.

The object hangs, defying gravity, I am beside it, looking down. I see my companion next to me below. I see the chamber we are in, then the compound, then the city.

The object seems like an image waiting for recognition, and I its carrier. I move away, leaving it alone.

Then with a huge eruptive force, like the first creation of all time, a brilliant light spreads its winged glow in all directions, filling space, like a thought filling the entire sky, which is now again imprinted on the dome, and lit with the fire of the sun.

I see shapes moving through the cloisters of the Abbey Church.

Others stand beside Parliament. Silent, ready.

Another group form a circle around the Foreign Office, Downing Street, and the Ministry of Defence.

Armed guards stand by, but see nothing, know nothing. The sensors register nothing.

The lights in the church fade. Guards move to and fro, trying to find the cause. There is panic. Then a temporary peace.

I turn and see a window on eternity. Stars are moving, comets passing, whorls of space-objects in a complex of mingled light.

I cover my eyes. The room shakes. I sink to the ground, fighting with my remaining strength.

I wipe away tears, hold my hands against my head.

I hear the rushing wind, the torments of empty space in the eternal void, the cries come at me from the souls of the sacrificed.

The new sun burns away their tears, even where they reside below.

Never again. I swear to the three figures that I will do everything I can to prevent it, for they are on the move again. They will have revenge.

"When the hurly-burly's done; when the battle's lost and won."

I hear them again. The screams out of the fire. The object falls to the ground.

In its centre a window appears, as in a crystal ball.

I see an island. The turbulent sea lashes its sides. In the centre of the island is a stone circle. In the centre of the circle stands a single tall stone.

Beneath the stone lies a vast chamber, deep beneath the surface. In the chamber stands a huge shape, pointing to the sky. About it figures, of different sizes, move like ants.

The Island! The place from which Mr Rummage saved Burnchester, and wanted me to reach. This is the site the figures want to find. We can be saved!

"I hear them!" I shout. "They are close by!"

I get up. The lady's face is ashen.

"Who? Who have you seen? What have you seen?"

"They are everywhere. We are surrounded. Like Burnchester. The enemy. Hurry. Let us go. Can we find a way out, without being seen? Hurry! It is our only chance. I must reach the Island before they do. I must take the recording of what I have seen."

The light returns. The images disappear. The cell lies in the pouch on the belt on the ground. The Sacred Cell.

There is a loud knocking.

I put the belt back on.

My companion's kind face reaches out to me.

The door opens.

Figures line up against the wall, watching.

I am not afraid. The lady turns.

I look at her, questioningly.

The figures move towards us.

Everything is but an image beneath which only the eyes of souls can see. There is nothing but eternity beyond. The image is what stands between us and emptiness, the emptiness of eternity, the "boom" of an empty frame.

I must seek the Image Maker, and with his or her help find the cell's home, and let it grow, into whatever shape it will.

If the enemy steals it, they take me too. They will haunt me until the goal is reached and then the battle will be for the soul of the world. The music will guide me.

The figures seem benign souls.

My companion smiles, as from a distant time. Her robes have changed. She carries another object familiar to me. It is a cup.

The image fades.

The figures let us pass as we walk towards the door. Their looks are haunted with eternal doubt.

"These are lost souls and seek our help. We must do so or they will seek the help of others."

"How?"

"Give them the freedom to follow as they will. It will help them back to life."

I bow to them as I pass. I beckon them to follow, which they do, becoming invisible, to most eyes.

"They are your hidden protectors. Look after them."

The woman takes a disc from one of the machines.

"We will study the recordings at a later time. You are right, we must hurry."

I take her hand. There is mutual warmth.

"I want to know more about you. You remind me of my dad in many ways. I am an orphan now, and though I am not old, I have experienced.... certain things. I wish I had been kinder."

My companion looks at me with eyes as rich as autumn leaves. I see her face for the first time beneath its mask and understand.

A smile builds across my face.

"Are you....?"

The lady smiles too.

"I am."

I throw my arms around her neck, unguarded now, tears pouring down my face, as I hug my Aunt Jane.

*

Dr Bartok and his guard retrace their steps up the stairs.

# 8

"Why didn't you tell me at the outset? Your disguise is brilliant."

"We have been well trained!"

I laugh aloud. It is the laughter of being with someone I have always loved, and who has watched over me.

I become serious again.

"I feel powerless. Nothing but a pawn, in someone else's game."

"You may feel that, but you have the power to accept, and the power to allow others to do the same for themselves. It isn't a game.

People who think that they are in charge of their own destinies are mostly deceived and often unhappy. Having seen a glimpse of the country far ahead – you saw the familiar shape and star – you cannot go back. And what is more, others, including your father, would not want it."

"My father?"

"Remember, he is my brother. He knew that you would be needed. He also knew that you would be ready."

"Am I?"

"Are any of us? Come, you must prepare."

Being with my aunt has given me strength.

"Help will come to you along the way. Have faith. I have something to show you."

In my mind's eye, I remember what I have just seen. I wish I had never had this power. But the power of insight is never secure.

I remember the Island and the life below ground. And the star. Calling me.

We head towards the room where I collect my things. Rompy jumps up, and sits beside me.

Some food has been laid out for me.

"You must eat something before you leave. It will be a long journey."

I ask her about my father's accident.

"It was a long time ago. It was never fully solved. All we know is that he disappeared in suspicious circumstances. We may never know what really happened."

Shortly, we enter a series of rooms, containing monitoring equipment, at which several women sit. One of them greets my aunt anxiously.

She reports that the Abbey Church has been infiltrated. The route we came in by is blocked. Some force is preventing movement.

"Then we must go another way."

We hurry along a labyrinth of corridors.

I ask about the Order of the Magdalene.

"I heard Mr Rummage or Mr Baxter mention it. They are something to do with The Knights Templar, and the lost secrets. Are they important?"

She says that the order is a cover for something else. Like most things.

We go out of a side door and down some concrete steps to a small entrance which my aunt opens with a key.

We exit into a walled garden.

Beyond the wall we hear security personnel giving instructions over a loud-hailer, for everybody to leave the area. Doors bang, a low siren echoes in the precinct.

We hurry across the grass to a door close to the north wall

of the Great Abbey Church, against which there is scaffolding.

I hear footsteps in the shadows. I look up and notice familiar shapes against the stone-climbing irons!

"They appeared in the last few months. They have appeared elsewhere, as they did at your school. It was this that alerted me to them."

My aunt lifts the medallion that hangs about her neck.

The Abbey Church seems to sway above me. I look down, trying to focus on something close to me.

We move into the cloister, around a courtyard containing a beautiful fountain, visible through the arches. I can hear murmuring, the singing of the monks who shadow this place.

My aunt pauses.

"Beneath the fountain is a chamber. In it are hidden ancient Christian relics, from long before the founding of the Abbey Church. Among them is the ring of Mary, from which the insignia on the medallion comes.

The insignia was made by the Great Image Maker. He or She who can draw down energy from the stars. The GIM has made an object which has the power to release and transmute energy in its own right. Only the GIM has the capacity to make images that last for a thousand years."

"Who is the Great Image Maker?" I ask.

"The GIM appears human, but in his and her work, which is of course not only his, but from a higher authority, he touches something beyond him and us, yet of ourselves."

I ask where the GIM can be found. My aunt replies that he dwells in a secret and sacred place, the deepest and darkest shadows, and normally only appears when and to whom he chooses, but that he has recently been imprisoned by the Dark Master, who tricked him. The Dark Master wants him to be his servant, but the GIM can only work according to his own rules. His services cannot be bought. This the Dark Master cannot understand. It is the same with the cell.

"I only hope we can get to him in time before he dies."

"Dies?"

"Yes. For though the Great Image Maker has the potential for eternal life, he needs people to love him. Nothing is complete without love. Nothing valuable is possible without it, especially if it is born of a higher energy. Love has many disguises too. The Image Maker has been dormant for a long time, but he is awake and we must find him, though he is trapped and sad. He was once captured by the Church, but that was a long time ago."

"We?"

"As I told you, there are others on the journey, some of whom you will know."

"Jules?"

My aunt smiles.

"He is part of the story too."

When I ask about herself, she explains that she had come from another part of the country, and had travelled to many lands, places far away, though she returned to the city, and stayed for some months from time to time, over many years, because it is where people most need her.

She explains that her work here is important but not her main task. It is just a temporary cover. One of many. She moves about the city, guiding those who seek, as needs arise. People come to her. She never seeks people out. She lives in the shadows. They come when the moment is right.

"Who comes to you? What do they want? Where do they find you?"

"You found me, didn't you?"

"Not exactly. I sort of arrived by chance."

"Is that what it was?"

I thought a little. I pieced together some of the parts of my journey. The first day I cycled to Burnchester with Jess, and then everything that followed. I saw that most of my actions followed a path not entirely chosen by me. Often I was following instructions, sometimes my instincts. Once the mystery had started at Burnchester, everything else, pretty much, followed. It made me quite frightened.

It seemed I had no choice but to follow. I fought with myself over this. I tried to persuade myself that I could turn back now. Of course I could. I could throw the cell away, give it to my aunt, and live happily ever after somewhere where I would not be known. But I didn't. Perhaps I couldn't.

I wanted to know about many things, most of all what had really happened to my father. I felt there was only one way I could do that: continue along the path that I had been given. That I, in part, had made.

"What do they want, these people, when they come to you?"

"They want to know what will happen to them. Like you. I study them, I ask them questions, I make a star map – not the silly kind that you read in papers – but something deeper that stretches back to the beginning. I answer them according to the questions they ask. There are others who I also study, who do not come, but who I study nonetheless."

"Who?" I ask. "How do you know about them?"

"The forces behind people who do not belong to time, and invade individuals for their own purposes until the individuals think they are the Gods.

I watch and listen to the currents. The stars too. That is why the cell is so important. It is pointing to something as yet unborn, but whose presence we can feel, and whose arrival we await. Remember where it came from."

"And the Power? The Energies?"

"Yes, those too, are sacred."

We turn left, then up some stairs before continuing straight on. All this time she talks, stopping from time to time to listen.

On one occasion, she speaks to a security guard before continuing.

She pauses to look through one of the corridor windows, as if at some distant troubled land.

101

Her eyes seem to change their colour at will, or perhaps it is I that seem to perceive them differently.

The medallion about her neck changes colour too.

My aunt describes some of the people who are out to destroy, halt progress, plunge us back into the darkness, into an abyss of hatred and intolerance, that will wreak havoc and despair to millions across the country and across the world. The hatred of bigotry and the abyss of ignorance, sponsored by fear, exploited for power. People who believe that only they are right, to the exclusion of others.

They are everywhere stalking the landscape like a virus, ready to mutate and strike. They are the embodiment of one of the oldest forces in the universe – and will lead to the final battle. Orchestrated by the Dark Master, who, I think, you "know"?

I tell my aunt that I thought I had seen him emerge from the fire and again when in the Domed Chamber at school. She seemed to know already.

I tell her that I thought the enemy figures were working for him. Then I tell her about the Stranger.

She asks a few questions about him, and if I had seen him since arriving in London.

I tell her about my encounters. I want to tell her about Shingle Island but decide to wait.

"We are at a turning point," she says. "No, we are beyond the turning point.

We have entered a new age, but as at dawn, we cannot know what the day will bring, unless we connect the past and present with our imagined future, and learn from all three in order to grow. In order to do that, we have to die and be reborn. It is an eternal cycle, but with each wave the stakes are higher. They are now our very survival."

"How can we learn from the future?" I ask.

"The future as it once seemed, became the present. In the future landscape a few things appear, like towers and city walls, but most is obscure. We have to tread carefully, but as we do, the sun will rise, and the mist clear, and we will be able to see all around us, at least enough for the next part of the journey, for the cycle is endless, the cycle of birth and death.

And when the mist is cleared we will see a mountain far ahead. It will be crowned.... Yes, like a cross above a mountain range, linking certain peaks, which look like stars. That is when the journey really begins.

That is the importance of our imagination. The ability to think of the possible. This is the realm of the GIM. By looking at what might be, we can make efforts to avoid the worst. But other factors are involved."

"Other factors?"

"There will be a storm before the sun rises again. We have heard stories from many places, not with the same power as Burnchester, but other sites of great age and meaning, which have been invaded for the power they possess.

Secret forces are joining hands everywhere. Sponsored by the oldest force of evil known to humankind, older than the earth, waiting to regain power and destroy the light of truth, wisdom and beauty. It is enforced by bigotry and domination, and sometimes, even wears the cloak of orthodoxy, just as in the old days in Europe.

However, they are afraid.

Though few realise it, there is something deeper stirring; something beyond their control, which threatens their very foundation.

There is a deeper significance, a deeper search, which few have glimpsed, and is beyond their perception. The questionable basis upon which so many myths depend is certainly serious. But there is something else. Something stirring in the universe, something much vaster, an energy, a cosmic impulse, a universal power, long hidden, which is beginning to make itself felt in the fissures of human consciousness.

Mystics have long glimpsed at what some have called the eternal language, but the collective is now involved, and the collective operating together has enormous power.

It may unify in time, but it will destroy in the process. The danger is that the collective will attach itself to the wrong images. Individuals will suffer. And if people feel threatened they will revert to what is safe. The curious truth is that few people in power recognise what is truly going on, which is why they tinker at the edges and pretend to be in control."

Something in my aunt's words make sense to me, though I do not understand them all. I have felt this sensation before, during our debriefing, after the incidents at Burnchester, over the summer. They struck a chord in me, though their meaning would only be revealed in time. It was like poetry creating shapes and sensations, powerful but indistinct, of things to come. Echoes both forwards and backwards through time, of something emerging and fading simultaneously.

"One of those who understands is Mr Rummage, and a small group of colleagues. Their knowledge, as mine, is far from complete, but the new images are gradually taking shape. All they can do is follow the path that has been given to them. Your father too was involved, in ways that would surprise you.

Something of what they – including your father – have perceived has become known to the enemy. The consequences of their knowing more would be more threatening to some – the Church included – than most can imagine. The authorities have had hints, and are terrified, preferring not to know, though their hands may be forced, as they are now. They are lost. I say again: tinkering at the edges. Not by what has been asserted. Not even if proof can be found. People will believe the myth they want. But they are terrified of something more.

The enemy has many faces, like Mr Vespers and Mr Blakemore, whom you know. They have had a glimpse of what is happening but no more. The Dark Master is behind all of them, though they do not know it. Each is flattered into believing they are important when they are not. The only exception is the so-called Stranger. He and the Dark Master are deadly enemies. But they need each other. For the Dark Master cannot live long in this world, and works through others and through agents, mostly seekers of power and wealth. The Stranger hopes to rule this earth without him.

If they find the power that they seek and the deeper source that they are beginning to suspect – which I will do every-thing in my power to prevent – nothing will be able to stop them, and that will be the end."

I am near to tears. My aunt sees me reaction.

"I am sorry. Yes, I know. It is you who carry one of the secrets that they seek. That was insensitive of me."

She asks me about my own story, which I outline briefly, excluding our sea journey, which I keep back.

She asks many questions about the timing and the exact process of events that led up to what I described, and the details of the stand-off between the figures of darkness (as I called them) and the parents and teachers, and the figure of light, as well as the child. I tell her of the three figures in white in the background. I had not mentioned Tom, but she seemed to know him and I told her what the figure from the painting had said, as far as I could remember, which is not as well as I had hoped. I did not tell her what had happened to me since then, in the City Beneath the Sea, for I did not think she would believe me. I did not tell her how I had grown up and felt ashamed that Tom was really nothing to me now.

This was not wholly true, for grow as I might, grow as I had, frightened as I was of the journey ahead, his silent spirit spoke to me still, had kept the figures at bay in the darkness of the Domed Chamber, and had even held back the Dark Master, and gave me a kind of strength, strength in my belief in the capacity of my own wings. This made me think of Mr

Baxter and the poem that he quoted – "No bird soars too high, if it soars with its own wings".

I laughed aloud. Heavy and big as I had now become, I still nurtured a belief in the possibility of the memory of that night. The memory of flying. More words came back to me: "But he who kisses the joy as it flies, lives in eternity's sunrise."

My aunt tells me that out of the storm light will come, a just still light; a ray of hope; a hint of the sublime, a seed from which will grow an essence that can transform the world and give back the energy and life that is its due, so that the darkness can become again the light and "the stillness the dancing." We have to bring other energies to our aid. They are huge, but they need skill and patience. And courage.

"The object you carry is part of that – it is a sacred object that will help us to give birth to our futures, if the land can be found where the soil can allow it to grow. Remember who gave it to you. Remember the source. Remember what happened. There is a purpose."

"Where is this land? Is it where I am going?"

"Yes. But it is all about us too. Only we need some symbol, a new power to make us see. Perception is everything. That is the importance of the cell. With that will come the ability to draw forth the power. The power of the universe, for good. At the moment it is hidden, but it is waiting to be revealed."

I think again of the words "Hidden Universe: Secret Power". I remember the strange language and symbols, and our instructions. I take out a piece of paper that I carry with me and hand it to her.

She unravels the paper, and studies it.

She murmurs something aloud, not by repeating the words on the page, but with some additional words that seem to illuminate the meaning. I look at the paper, and as I do so, the words shine out, the starry image and the symbols seem to lift into the air, and hold there.

I look, amazed. Ahead of both of us for a moment, in front of my forehead, the mountains hang like the shape of stars. Then they speed forward, and upwards, and suddenly twist and turn into a spiralling vortex, through the cloister ceiling which is momentarily open, where there are the stars above, for both of us to see. The mountains speed upwards until they stand in the sky, like a new cosmic house, and then melt, and disappear. They are gone.

We head towards a set of steps, only this time they go downwards.

"Who is the Dark Master?" I ask.

"The shadow of the divine, the primordial power, the eternal dark."

We proceed, footsteps echoing behind us. Over tombs of the long dead. Monks from former times. Memorial plaques just visible in the dim light.

We hear a choir which reminds me of the chanting in the Domed Chamber, when we were prisoners there. What could link the heavenly and the demonic, the terror of the Dark Master's disciples, and this divine music, I seek to know.

We pass stony walkways, the footsteps delayed, as if in distant harmony. I expect to see faces in the recesses on either side.

I wonder if the silent friendly figures follow.

I remember the tunnel that Jess and I followed in our escape from the Stranger.

Now the figures are close by. Those we had seen before whisper softly, as if they would be reincarnated. Perhaps they are uncertain, or afraid. Perhaps they were put to death. I wish that I had the power to help. I tell them I will if I can.

*

I hear the words of a poem that we once read.

Perhaps the words help me to access my thoughts, or

give them shape, as if they might be completed through the memory of others. Perhaps they are important for the journey.

"She walks in beauty, like the night
Of cloudless climbs and starry skies;
And all that's good of dark and light
Meet in the aspect of her eyes:
Thus mellow'd to that tender light
Which heaven to gaudy day denies."

Or is it?

"And all that's best of dark and bright
Meet in her aspect and her eyes."

Behind these shaded words others follow like my own shadow, in the captive places of the imagination, like the groves where spirits dwell. You will know them reader. I am drawn to them.

Struggle to release them, so that they can go I know not where and lead us to places from which no traveller returns.

Out of nowhere it seems, my school world appears before me, as if to remind me of what has passed. The remembered images of both good and bad – the delight of innocence and the greying tremor of recent fears will live forever in my mind. I long to walk on its sacred grounds again.

*

I stop at some relief work carved upon the cloister wall.

Four figures sitting around a tomb hold up cards. They seem to be its guardians. At the angle three of them sit, I can see what is contained on their cards.

Each card carries a symbol. Together the symbols seem to form conjunctions or other aspects which I think must be astrological. They are like some of the images from the book in Burnchester library.

On the tomb in front of them is a globe. It could be a seer's crystal ball, it could be the world. It could be a cell. The three figures whose cards I see have small piles of coins beside them, except that I do not think they represent money, rather hours. The fourth figure, who sits above the others at the far side of the tomb, holds a hand that nobody can see. It has no coins, or hours, yet it seems to be winning. He or she - from a certain angle he is a man, from another, a woman – smiles ambiguously. He or she holds a card up, and is about to let it fall.

Behind the card is a mirror, forever hinting at the hand that is visible only to eternity. The figure holding the card reminds me of the figure in the painting at Burnchester – the figure that dissolved.

Beneath the figure's foot, I see a serpent. In it I see the face of the Dark Master and try to shy away. Yet the serpent itself is not evil.

Behind the tableau, in the background both above and below ground, I make out the outlines of three figures in white, shadowing the whole scene. One I had seen on Shingle Island. All were at Burnchester.

We pass scaffolding reaching high above the buttresses of the Great Church.

We proceed down a side cloister.

I want to ask my aunt so much, but there is no time. There is never, time. Better to follow the path, a path, and allow the journey to provide glimpses of that eternal language that we cannot simply appreciate in deeds.

"The Magdalene was a companion to Jesus. Some say she was his wife. Some people go further and claim that she is the mother of Jesus' children.

Even some priests, as, I feel sure, does the Reverend Sandals."

My aunt holds the medallion about her neck and continues.

"This was once blasphemy, for which many have died, over the centuries. Many see the return of the Magdalene as the return of the feminine to her rightful place in the balance of energies that drive our universe and inspire our reverence.

Others see it as a gradual process of subversion, so that all beliefs cascade into chaos. That is where the enemy is ready to take over.

But all this is too simple. The face of the feminine is many-sided. There is not just one image of her, any more than there is of man.

When the Dark began to reappear, I felt it through the medallion. It is, as you guessed, an insignia of the Order of the Magdalene, in so far as it exists.

It has many faces – some say thirteen – and can be recognised by those who know. Like all great images, it points to something else, because it comes from a hidden source, and is a means of leading us to that other place. It does not provide answers. Something lies beyond it, but we need it in order to start. Without it there is only emptiness.

Remember, the Order of the Magdalene is not what it seems."

I think of the symbol that formed on my cut face.

We reach what looks like an exit door. It is heavily barred.

I hear a tumult outside. A guard rushes in from a passage-way to the left.

"There has been a breach at the main gates. Someone inside the Great Church has disappeared. There has been an attack at the Church House, and several people have been injured, but there is more."

The guard whispers something in her ear.

There is barely a ripple on my aunt's face.

"I see," she says.

There is another loud crashing. The door breaks open and a woman bursts into the room.

".... Hurry, hurry. They are closing all the gates. Security have closed every exit and entrance. They will search every-where, the whole complex above and below ground, the whole community of the Abbey and its sacred grounds.

The Thames has breached its banks six miles downstream,

and there is fear of further breaches. More evacuations are imminent. Parliament is threatened."

"Take what you can and make sure everyone follows the procedure. I may be some time."

The woman leaves and my aunt takes my arm and walks me towards the door.

"Does that mean the whole of London is at risk?"

"The whole country."

We reach a side entrance to the Great Church.

Inside, the music and the light strike us like scented waves. The high roof is barely visible.

We pass the choir stalls, and the huge gold screen behind the altar, on which a cross would normally stand. But the cross is on its side. Beside it is an object in the shape of a fruit. One that I do not recognise. Forensic workers are covering the area, as if in shame.

Far above us towards the west door, a space is visible in the roof, where the stones fell. Workmen are putting up a high scaffold. I notice the end of a wire coming through the roof.

My aunt follows my eyes.

"Someone was nearly killed."

On the floor close to Poet's Corner, I see a circle of scattered objects like those in the Church of St Mary Magdalene, that disturbed the Reverend Sandals so deeply.

I recall the figures entering the church on the night of our first encounter. I sense their presence here. I hear murmuring. I ask my aunt what it is.

She listens but hears nothing. I am sure someone or something is chanting inside the Great Church, hidden from view. Or is it a vibration from below ground?

"Can anyone enter the church at night?" I ask.

"Only through the crypt, which has a secret entrance from a tunnel."

"Where does the tunnel go?"

111

"To the Palace of Westminster, and beyond. There are others that go elsewhere. They can only be reached from the crypt. I suppose something could have got in that way."

I look back at the cross. I see at its base, the slumped figure fallen in a woman's arms. The pieta.

The cross seems to be crying.

We cross the choir to another door, where a verger lets us pass.

We enter the night air, the traffic hurrying past. The huge Abbey Church above us like a giant sarcophagus.

There are police and soldiers everywhere.

"I must leave you here," my aunt says, looking into my eyes. "I have much to do. Be afraid of nothing, but be on your guard."

"Will we meet again?" I ask.

"When your need is greatest, call, and I will come. But only then."

My aunt takes the medallion from her neck and hands it to me.

"Wear it," she says, "and keep it safe."

Before I can speak, she says that she will communicate with me from time to time.

I quote the words, "Hidden Universe: Secret Power". She looks at me again, as if judging whether she should tell me more. She must have known much more about me than I realised.

"Supposing the Great Image Maker could find an image that would bring the world together, then he or she would lighten the world."

"If the enemy found the image – and the power to go with it – they would control the world, in fact the universe. That is why Mr Rummage's project is so important.

It is what your father was interested in.

It is possible that some church members will join the enemy, in order to protect themselves. Deals can always be made. The Church has a history. As do States. The Prime Minister, remember, is a believer."

I try to interrupt but am stopped.

My aunt added one more thing.

"In the Church at Burnchester there is a list of incumbents attached to the wall. Did you ever notice that the Reverend Sandals always pauses in front of it and makes the sign of the cross?"

I explained that I had.

"One of them, an old man, many years ago, claimed that he could fly. Just an image of course. But he was accused of black magic and of being in league with the devil."

I thought of the witches in Macbeth and of the instruments of darkness. I thought of the items on the floor of the church that Mr Vespers had made us clear up, and those that I had just seen. I thought of my own flight.

"He was burned at the stake."

I gave a scream, and put my hand to my face. I thought of all the screams that I had heard, of the people, from all faiths, who had died in the Reformation, and was struck with a pain like a Spear in the heart. God must be in a state of constant tears, if he exists at all.

I imagined souls rising from the ground, wherever there had been injustice.

I looked at her.

"There are many ways to fly," I whispered, remembering Tom's words.

"There are indeed. One day, not so far off, you will know more of his identity. Deo Concedente," my companion said.

"Whose?" I asked.

"The other person who could teach you about flying."

I looked at my aunt questioningly.

"Your father. It will come in useful. Remember there is not just one image of the feminine, any more than there is of Man."

She turns back and is lost in the night.

I place the medallion around my neck and hurry across the road, towards Downing Street.

Determined but afraid.

# 9

I could feel the situation worsening. We were looking into an abyss.

How long it would be before the enemy found me, I could not tell.

I just hoped I had enough time to reach the Prime Minister.

*

I look back at the security lights strafing the Abbey. The gash in the roof is like a scar.

Government, intelligence and faith seem like an ancient order in itself. Economic power is in another part of town.

Police stand in line across Parliament Square, into White-hall, down the Embankment. Troops take up position outside Parliament. Barricades are set up. Traffic is redirected.

*

At the back of Downing Street, snow falls on Rompy and me.

The Cabinet Offices are fronted with concrete. Basements are sealed.

Cameras everywhere. Democracy requires everyone to be a watcher, and so democracy is dying. Nothing escapes their attention except the real enemy, which cannot be seen.

Walls are topped with razor wire. Light filters out of windows, but most are dark.

The bells of the Abbey ring like the chimes at midnight. Big Ben competes. The two cannot agree. The balance swings from side to side, to the echoes from the graves of the dead, who suffered the consequences of the intolerance of both. Ruled by the King of this Earth who resides in another part of the city, and takes bets on the rate of change. In harmony it seems with the God of the Realm below.

Half-visible figures hide in doorways.

Downing Street. Security watch me approach, study my pass. Wait for the response to an eye scanner. There is some disagreement, but they let me through. Mr Veech has been thorough. I choke in his memory.

I reach the waiting journalists. There are TV crews from all over the world. News, like the virus, is spreading.

A Christmas tree stands between us and the door to Number 10.

The exit to Whitehall is to our right. The gates are three deep.

Inside the security cabin, an officer monitors an approaching car.

I look closely at the Prime Minister's house, planning how to enter.

Points of light reflect off its walls, like strokes of luminous paint, from high to low, forming the skeleton of a vertical line. They are evenly spread.

They glow and dim, but I can see them clearly, even against the snow. These are not lights.

"Alright. Rompy?"

A car swings towards Downing Street.

From the roof, an armed officer studies its arrival.

The barricades open. The car halts next to security.

116

Its door is opened by the entrance to Number 10.

A man steps out, and enters.

As he crosses the threshold he seems, perhaps arbitrarily, to turn. Does he pause, just for one split moment, in my direction?

Rompy is agitated. I gasp for breath.

He turns and the door closes.

I begin to choke. I have seen him before. Not long ago. He cannot have recognised me. Can he?

I begin to shake, uncertain whether to continue. My plans ruined.

"Are you OK?" a police officer asks.

I cannot answer.

"Anyone'd think you'd just seen a ghost!"

She offers me some water. I straighten, breathe slowly, and drink a little. I point to the door of Number 10.

I bend down again, in sharp pain. What seems like the point of a spear digs into my side. I must speak.

Without revealing my plan. Perhaps his arrival is my advantage.

The officer glances at a colleague.

The man who has just entered Number 10 is a sworn enemy of the State. Linked to the Darkest Forces. Here, at the centre of power. Why?

The second policeman checks images from his hidden camera.

I am short of breath.

"Are you sure you're OK? Would you like to sit down?" the policewoman says.

I bend to pat Rompy.

"I will tell the Prime Minister, no one else," I whisper to him.

"I'm OK, thanks," I say, looking up.

She notices the medallion about my neck.

"But I do have an urgent request. It is of great importance."

"What is it? A statement is due within the hour. That's why you're all here, isn't it?"

"I must speak to The Prime Minister."

The policewoman looks at me. At her colleague.

"I'm serious," I add. "I have an important message for him. Vital to national security."

I touch the medallion, which seems to emit pulses of light.

The line on the wall seems to respond.

The policewoman is thinking something through. She tells me that the Prime Minister is busy at the moment. If I could tell her what it is.

The policeman hears something over his radio. His expression changes. He checks a photo.

I look into the policewoman's eyes. There is something about my conviction, the energy that I project, that holds her.

I haven't much time.

The policeman calls her.

Rompy barks.

"OK. I'll write my message, then," I say.

I write two words on a piece of paper, and give it to the policewoman.

"Will you make sure the Prime Minister gets it? It's vital. I hope it's not too late."

Reluctantly, she reads it. Then every ounce of humour leaves her face. She shows it to her colleague.

"Impossible! He's one of the Prime Minister's closest advisers."

"The man who has just gone in – is a traitor. He is behind the Burnchester incident and the destruction at.... Shingle Island. London is next. We have not long to wait. They're here now!"

The officers confer. They think I am mad.

I stare at the strips of light on the wall, still emitting pulses of light.

The incongruity of it.

I follow the lines of the building in front of me; every window, every ledge, every pipe, trying to work something out. I know another way. Another way to get in.

I step back. I sense the figures about to move against me, against us all. I must go. Now.

"Will you make sure the Prime Minister gets it? Thank you."

The policewoman nods, uncertainly.

Before she can speak, I hasten away, behind my colleagues, quickening my pace.

They must not take me in.

The points of light. The little elements that seem to hang there like forbidden fruit on a dying tree, are climbing irons.

As I exit, another car arrives from Whitehall. A second man gets out.

I hurry away.

*

Inside Number 10, people are on high alert.

The ticking of the hall clock seems to be beating more than time.

Inside the Cabinet Room the Head of the Security Service is speaking.

"The situation, ladies and gentlemen, is deteriorating rapidly.

There has been a serious breach in security at the Abbey Church next door. A full alert is in operation.

There have been threats to the House this very afternoon.

The girl we have been following, last seen in East London yesterday, has gone missing.

The Americans, the Russians, the Chinese have had similar incidents, and are blaming each other. Such a breach in our defences must have a cause. This is beyond the Priory.

Yet nobody can explain it.

The State is under severe and imminent threat. They may even be around us now."

There is a knock at the door. A man goes over to the Prime Minister with a message. The Prime Minister's eyes flicker.

"Please continue."

"Shingle Island is one of our most important, and secret, monitoring stations. All data transmission systems have gone down. All information has ceased. Without it Doonwreath cannot survive for long."

"And if that fails?"

"Our defences would cease. It would be more than a declaration of war. It would be a virtual admission of surrender."

The Heads of MI5 and MI6 exchange glances. There is something more, something not being disclosed.

The Head of Government Communications speaks.

"The press is having a field day. They have had nothing to go on but speculation. We have all seen the corps outside here, outside every ministry, even outside our own houses. Unless we give them a coherent story they will add to the panic, and probably destroy the government anyway. Confidence is ebbing, and confidence is the key. If we can maintain it for a short while, we may pull through. But it is very, very close. We cannot deceive people for ever. It may be too late as it is."

The Prime Minister scans a few of the headlines on the table in front of him.

"Invasion by unseen enemy." "Aliens' secret invasion." "UFOs land."

"In effect, ladies and gentlemen, unless we do something, we will be taken over."

"Put a D notice on the press."

"It wouldn't work, and it's not enough. We have to find answers fast."

"How is it that this man Veech can continue reporting? Bring him in. He might give us a lead."

"Mr Veech was found dead this afternoon, with two incisions to his throat."

"Do we know who was responsible?"

"The mark of the Priory was on his neck."

"God bless him."

"And the girl?"

"She is our top priority. She may tempt the enemy out of its lair. And may hold the clue to our survival."

The Prime Minister turns to the Defence Chief.

"And the loss of Burnchester?"

"Has been a disaster, Prime Minister. It was a central source of power, throughout the system. Though not predictable, it has been an essential component in the defence of the realm for a very long time. It was instrumental in our defeat of the enemy in World War 2. It is instrumental in combating the forces of the Dark today. Without it Shingle Island could not operate, and Doonwreath will soon fail."

"So an attack there might not even be necessary?"

"We have a reserve, but it has not been tested. We will keep Doonwreath operational as long as we can. The enemy does not know of the reserve. They will attack anyway."

"And.... the Spearhead?"

The Intelligence Chiefs share glances.

"For Heaven's sake, this is not a game! Nothing in this room is off our radar."

The head of MI5 speaks.

"Mr Rummage and his team have been studying its capability for some time. It seems that the Spearhead, or belief in it, allows other forces, including those at Burnchester, to be tapped – how we don't know. The Spearhead is key to their release.

Hence the interest from groups such as the Priory.

But the results of Mr Rummage's most recent research are not available, and without him I cannot give you a full answer. I have had hints, but I do not know. Other elements, besides the Spearhead, seem to be involved. Material and, perhaps, mental."

"How can a single man be working outside our own security screen?"

"It is difficult to monitor someone of his expertise, which is unique. Besides, sometimes, we have to trust."

She is lying.

"What else has he been working on? Mental you say? You said that the girl may hold the clue."

"Mr Rummage, as you know, is a distinguished physicist. He has been seeking other forms of energy, and methods of energy release. The Spearhead, given that it exists – and that is not certain – might be superceded by something else. Of even greater, perhaps darker, power. Power that may not be controllable, from deep in the universe."

The Prime Minister waves for her to continue.

"Mr Rummage would no doubt have let us know in due course. But he has disappeared, along with his colleagues. So have the alien figures. I presume, underground. The girl may carry an important clue.

If the enemy reach Doonwreath, they will try to destroy it, or operate it for their own purposes, but the power they need may yet be beyond them. If, that is, the Spearhead is no longer what it was, or has been superceded by something else. However, we may have lost it to the enemy already."

"What you are saying is: either way we may be destroyed. It's only a matter of when."

"No. One offers hope, the other doesn't."

The Prime Minister turns to an assistant, who goes out.

"To whom or what do you ascribe the capture of Burnchester and loss of Shingle Island?"

"Something beyond our understanding or capability. We do not know who or what. Something bigger than all of us."

There is a knock at the door. The assistant enters, followed by two men, whose faces we cannot see.

I hurry through the darkness, like the fog in Bleak House, leaving Number 10 behind. It is my only chance.

Above, a helicopter beats in the gloom.

I chant the words "Hidden Energy; Secret Power."

Perhaps the climbing irons are an energy conduit, or a communication system, from the depths or the skies?

We are witnessing the start of an invasion.

Two police cars wait.

Rompy looks across to the park. The lake reflects the dark. There is a rustling of leaves. People trudge over the bridge through the blanket of white, like ghosts on the mantle of the moon.

"Rompy! Stop pulling! What's the matter?"

I study the buildings carefully.

*

Not far away flood warnings howl. Big Ben strikes.

Along the North Sea, coast guards prepare for the worst. Toxic canisters from an unknown source, strike the beaches and break open.

Incident rooms are being set up, as the threats increase.

From the military base close to Dunemoor, another force is being monitored. It stems from Shingle Island, something as yet undefined. An energy the watchers have not encountered before.

The radar screens at RAF Marham and Wattisham have recorded unidentified intrusions into their air space for the third time in as many days. These "objects", appear as a line of dots, stay, move sharply, then vanish.

There have been sightings inland, close to Rendlesham Forest.

The sightings are analysed by the Ministry, in vain. US

intelligence confirms them, but have no answers. All stations are on red alert. The entire air might of the Western Alliance is primed.

Two local ufologists, having gone out the previous night, are found dead in the morning.

Others along the coast, including Mr Greenshank, have seen unusual lights in the sky.

The Prime Minister and the President have been informed.

It is a matter of record that, before his disappearance, Mr Rummage had evidence of similar activity. Records of his calls to Doonwreath, the secret monitoring station, confirm this. Something momentous is happening in the universal order.

*

The true meaning of unfolding events is understood by no-one of this earth, though a small handful have had a glimpse. These few – notably Mr Rummage and his team – are required to be silent.

*

A feeling haunts me like the cast-off coat of a Fisher King.

The gates at the back of Downing Street swing open and four police riders exit. Two black cars follow with four riders behind.

The cars swing right, then turn towards the Palace.

I see the sign I am looking for: the Cabinet War Rooms.

I pull Rompy to my side and glance about me. This is my chance.

I walk over to the entrance.

Inside the door a face – a face in pain – looks at me, as if beckoning. It is like the image in a portrait. Then it turns its eyes to the floor and begins to fade.

I give the door a push. It opens.

"You can't go in there...." I imagine someone saying.

"But there's somebody in there.... I thought I saw a face."

A security guard stands behind me.

"What face?"

"In the window of the door."

"Hop it, before I report you!"

I walk on.

*

Nobody else seems to see them, the faces. Perhaps I am mad.

I turn to the moon. I wonder what it sees. I wonder what God must think, looking down all the time, on us. His and Her creation.

The stars above seem to be following me. I look up again, wondering. As I look, shadows move nearby, just as the stars take on a special shape. A shape I recognise, of an actual mountain range.

One day, mankind will be up there, colonising. Already there are advanced plans, secret plans that occasionally get into the press. The Americans, the Russians, the Indians, the Chinese, the Japanese, and others. Working to go into deep space. For themselves or for humanity? Or are we already there? Somebody or something?

Will it make any difference? For instance, make us better people? Would we still burn our toast for breakfast?

Would it just be us again, up there instead of down here? The same old us, or almost the same. Evolved a bit, but not much, like in a dance. Moving on the same floor. Unless we can leave evil behind. Only take the good. A new order. There is no light without the dark.

Anyway, it's still a dream. We don't have the technology. We don't have the power.

They are trying to overcome the difficulties, preparing for

the sacrifices, inevitable, in any change, involving progress. The words "Hidden Universe: Secret Power" come to me again. Just as other words do, though I don't ask them. These words come from a different source than within my own head, wear different masks. People talk, make things up. The stories become myths, are believed in and secured, then, much later, are unravelled. Once Mars showed no evidence of water. Now it does. "Truth can never be told so as to be understood and not believed."

\*

A car screeches past. Nearly hits me.

I jump back at the last second. Catch my breath. I am losing control, wandering onto the road. I used to be so focused. I am giving in to forces beyond me. Perhaps that is the only way. To protect the Sacred Cell, or find the Spearhead.

I might have been killed.

A head looks out of the car window and bellows. The car roars on.

I turn. Behind me, a beam of light falls from the door of the Cabinet War Rooms. It wasn't there before.

The police seem to have disappeared. No security guard. Nothing but the light beyond the door, from where had I seen the face.

The Cabinet War Rooms.

A light is on inside. There must be someone there. I haven't much time. The clock is closing on its doom hour.

I think of tunnels beneath the city. Some say they go on for miles, even across country. Perhaps they go to Burnchester, perhaps around the world. About as absurd as saying there is water on Mars.

I check that the cell is carefully hidden.

I push the door and enter.

The air is dry with a familiar energy.

As if time has paused.

There is light coming from behind the desk and whistling from below the stairs to the right.

I sense the wretched innocence of the country's "finest hour". Its relevance for me now. Something here will change my journey forever.

I lean over the desk and call.

"Hello!"

"Hello!" a voice answers.

I stand silently a moment, surprised.

"Is anybody there?"

There is just a faint echo.

The whistling has become a low warble, above the clumping sound as of furniture being moved about.

I look into the ante-room. There are coats behind a curtain, and a sealed cardboard box on the floor. A kettle in the corner.

On the desk is a table of entry prices and guide books for sale: 'London during the Blitz'; 'Churchill's Secret Command Centre'.

I take an audio guide.

The season, the great solid walls and the sounds from below seem rather haunting. They remind me of something, someone.

I hear a hurried "ticking".

I walk to the staircase.

It is here, over fifty years ago, that the Defence of the Realm was orchestrated, with the austere mixture of tragedy and heroism, like a cauldron of destiny. The Prime Minister, the War Cabinet and support staff, had lived and worked here.

Their presence hangs in the air.

I hear other sounds. The entire place is coming alive, given life by the whistling; like my mother's music.

I hear the Prime Minister's voice – as I recall it on the record played by my father – the speeches that moved me, even as a young child, beyond grief: transforming and magical, reconciling time with destiny. Like the incantation, but for good, that Mr Blakemore practised.

The door behind me opens.

"All OK?" A uniformed officer calls.

There is a moment's silence. He hears the whistling, and leaves.

*

For a moment I am back at Burnchester.

I see the carved names of agents on the Folly; the ghost-like figures close to the place where they were air-lifted into the night sky.

In a rare alchemical moment of clarity, the jumbled events there; the terrors of Bonfire Night, and all the stories and briefings, appear to me in a moment, and the purpose of Burnchester, as a source of transforming, perhaps mystical, power, is inscribed on my imagination like diamond light.

It is this, with the Spearhead as a symbol, that is the basis of the school's existence. It is the insight, and the universal power for which Burnchester is a co-ordinate across the world, linked to the potency of the Spearhead that gives it its significance. And I, without realising it until now, despite the task that I have been given, have been trained in some of its arts. I am beginning to think that perception is key.

I recollect the Dome flooded in glorious light. I see the ancient figures cast upon the ceiling, symbols of the search for truth and salvation; the place where the Spearhead had seemed to appear, and where that mysterious word in its ambiguous glory, was written.... 'Muchbuhijushin'. The whole spectacle of past and present, light and dark, where the evil figure had been nearly born, fused into one with the light that destroyed it. I think of the cross-sword that I had thrown away, and that has been found. I am ready to pay the price, whatever the consequences.

I stand in the very place that I had stood on that fateful day, feeling the story all about me. I stand on the lawns beside the hall, and look up at the tower that Newton had used, bathed in sunlight. I see the mist rise from the river basin up over the fields, shrouding the hidden figures.

Everything that had happened to me there is resurrected in this moment, and, as I stand close to the stairs, multiple images, all at once, arise. From this past can I see the future too?

Is this the ability to fly, that I had lost, and have now regained?

Is this the capacity that I must develop and control for the benefit of the meaning of the cell? Is this the training that I had only half-consciously undergone?

For I can traverse the landscape of Burnchester with absolute clarity in forensic detail, almost at will, and see everything as if I were there, the things I seek. This is my gift. To visit places that most people never visit or retrieve. To travel, at will, over time and space. Reader, it is yours too.

Give shape to the wings of memory, not just my own. Bring the past and present together, and trace the journey forward, to take me onward. Travel with the eye of mind – as in Shakespeare's phrase – build up the picture from the fusion of the imagination and the reality, to give me the ability to seek out and find secrets hidden in places far and wide. These are my tasks.

The moment and the subject, and the search, are not in my control.

*

I descend the stairs.

Ahead of me is a desk snugged into an alcove, and doors leading off to the left and right.

Through one of these, I can see a larger room which looks

like a library. By the door is a desk on which objects are displayed.

I check my audio guide, type in the reference number on the wall by the door, and enter.

As I look around me I become attuned to the energy.

I pass wall posters and arrows pointing in the direction of the Cabinet Room, the Strategy Room, the Map Room, the Communications Room.

I reset the number on my audio hand-set. "This is the BBC Home Service...."

Faded red arrows point upwards to a set of stairs. Another arrow points to a dormitory chamber underground. I stand at the top of the steps looking down, but decide against it.

I pause at the canteen, whose walls are covered with black and white photos of the Blitz: people in an underground bomb shelter, packed like tarnished treasure; smoke-filled skies over the Dome of St Paul's, streaked with beams of light. A ghastly mix of animation and death; smashed vehicles outside the ruins of homes, people dead or dying. Endless pain. Intransigent hope. The Prime Minister there. The then present.

We are at war, someone has said. Even now. Mr Rummage had almost said it. Not the same war, but another. Mr Rummage's virus, the haunted figures, the unknown enemy, creeping over the dark, ready and willing, in correspondence with ancient myths, exploiting current fears, infiltrating, deceiving, and on the move. Closer and closer to their ultimate goal: power. I stare in my mind's eye at the dead on Shingle Island. But they are not the enemy we think.

The Priory are close to the Spearhead. The empty frame even now shows, in its surround, the lost fragment which had given them a clue.

The Dark Master's shadow and voice hang in the air, like an estranged black dog, reminding me of Titan. The Priory had sought the Spearhead, even in those dark war days.

*

It was the symbol that kept hope alive, and the enemy have nearly found it, perhaps have found it. They know that Tyro carries an object more important still, though only in its pre-embryonic stage, a holy image in the making.

*

I remain alert. I feel the tension between hurrying and the importance of now. I must find a secret way into the Prime Minister's office. But I must read the signs here, which might guide me on my journey.

I can hear sirens. Are they outside, or part of the images of a restored history? I can hear the sounds of voices in a meeting. The sonorous voice of the Prime Minister. Advocacy, retort, un-compromise. Masks of language and tone, orchestrated personalities like instruments of mind.

I wonder on whose side I would be, moving with one voice and then another. Perhaps I could be them all. Multiple identities, multiple masks.

A corridor leads off to my left.

"Rompy, this way!"

There seems to be someone coming. Is it a trick of the light?

# 10

To my right a short corridor leads into another room, which I enter.

"Rompy!" I call. "Where are you? Come here! At once!"

On the far side of the room, to my surprise, a man is leaning over a table. He seems to be preparing something. He stops whistling. He must have heard me.

"You're early!" the man says, looking round. "Doesn't start for another half-hour."

I look at him, his head facing the table again. He checks that each place has paper and pen and that there is water.

"You're cheerful!" I hear myself say.

"Gotta be, as the PM says. This is our darkest hour. Might not be here tomorrow. Remember his words: "If you're going through hell, keep going!" Go and get yourself a cuppa.... I would."

"What are you preparing for? Who are you?"

The man chuckles.

"Go on with you!"

I leave the War Room. Within a few moments, I find the Map Room. There is a vibration in the air, as if from a generator.

I look through the perspex security glass and see the desks covered in papers, and the telephones in a row, in various colours. One, a direct line to the President in Washington. I am reminded of the rooms in the tunnels at Burnchester.

132

The ashtrays have been emptied, but there is sugar still in the bowl. There are papers and files on some of the tables beside lamps, and on the wall a huge map of the Atlantic. Each pin-hole signifies the loss of a ship. I type the room number onto my audio-guide and listen.

Without thinking, I walk through the perspex glass.

I find the team busy at work.

There are solemn phone conversations: to the Admiralty; Central Command; the President. Sometimes the tone is a confidential murmur, at others a forced engagement, dramatic, angry. There are sighs, even laughter. Every modulation of speech, every level of receptivity. Intermingled, it is like a symphony. With a backdrop of potential despair.

Two people are busy at the wall map, adding a flag at the news of a lost ship. Occasionally a skull and crossbones is placed where an enemy ship has been sunk. There is a muted cheer. A sadness at others' death.

Another map shows the United Kingdom. It is marked with airfields, military installations, camps and troop movements. A few sites are highlighted. One of these is Burnchester. I look closely at it. It is ringed with concentric circles extending outwards, just like in the tunnels.

On the wall is a clock. The time is approaching midnight.

I can hear the crackle of a speaker in the corner of the room.

A tea lady comes round. The tinkle of crockery and the whispered thanks add to the mystery.

The whining of a siren sharpens the click of typewriters. Someone cracks a joke. There is the snatch of laughter, like a safety catch. Work resumes. It will be all night, as it is every night.

Until the enemy is destroyed. Or we are destroyed.

I ask if I can help, but nobody responds. It is as if I should already know what to do. So I busy myself at a table with a telephone extension to the BBC studio along the corridor.

I listen to the murmur of voices, unravelling the words, to see what I can learn. People look up at me from time to time.

My telephone rings.

"No, there have been no new briefings. I'll ring back!"

I feel an energy flow through me, as it has never done before. I feel at home. The war of long ago is over; but continues along different lines. "We have scotched the snake, not killed it." The instruments of darkness are on the move again and the stakes are higher.

The phone rings again.

"Hello? Hello?" I say.

The hideous thunder of a bomb resonates from outside. The building shakes. The Abbey Church precinct has been struck. There is screaming, sirens whine again. The smell of smoke mingles with death.

The voice on the phone shouts, but I cannot hear.

Someone calls out "Bastards!" People carry on, their determination greater.

I notice a door into the next room.

I am about to hang up, when the voice becomes clear, an agitated voice – it is a man's.

He tries to speak, but the voice fades again. As if drugged, or injured. He seems far away. He knows my name.

"Who is this?" I shout, standing up.

Everyone looks up.

"Tyro. I haven't got long. It's me, Veech. This is the only line open. The last train north leaves at nine. Make sure you are on it. Things are moving to a head. Head for the Island. I was at the Abbey Church, remember.... Goodbye and good luck!"

I hear a terrible scream.

"Mr Veech!"

The line goes dead. My head spins. I can't focus. I feel sick.

I make my way towards the door. I remember his dead face.

Ahead of me is a map of the British Isles, a large map

of continental Europe and West Asia, one of North Africa.

Others join them to form one of the whole world. Across them are various symbols, of troop movements, supply lines, battle positions.

A few places are highlighted as epicentres, with concentric circles around them, as with Burnchester. A valley in South West France, an island off the north coast of Scotland. There are occasional sites in other continents.

I stand back.

I wonder if I can travel with my mind's eye to any of the places. I choose one and try to concentrate.

I imagine how big the map would have to be to cover our solar system, our galaxy, the universe. And how big our minds to see it all.

This was the universe then.

I remember flying high above the earth as in a dream, and seeing the contours of the world fade into the distance as I climbed higher into space. I remember seeing country boundaries increase and retract. Places of worship arise and fall like the beat of an ancient heart. I remember the dark visions in the recent dome. Whilst in pursuit of the three figures, by moonlight, I could also see the shapes that lay beneath the earth.

I could see, beneath the Stranger, a shape of such darkness, which, like a black hole, might consume humanity in its greed.

Attached to the maps is a symbol, of beauty and simplicity. It is like a cross, perhaps a sword, perhaps even a spearhead. It emits intense power. My medallion seems to respond.

The maps seem to shimmer. Different pulses of energy appear to arise from the special sites. They come and go, rise and fall, like the changing fortunes of war, like the rise and fall of civilisations. Who is the enemy now?

Beneath each pulse is some other energy, more powerful

than the rest, like a gamma ray, that emanates from them, co-ordinates of certainty, that hold the world together, yet coming, it seems from somewhere else, although through specific places on the map. "Whoever holds the Spearhead will rule the world".

Is this the Secret Power?

I walk up to the map.

I focus on a place in the Highlands of Scotland, hidden in cavernous mountains, close to the sea. There seem to be heavy defences close to it, even though it is so isolated. It seems not to be of this world at all. Not far distant is an Island, on which is marked a set of standing stones called the Ring of Loth.

The place is called Doonwreath. The energy from here is overwhelming.

It is there that Mr Rummage has told me to go.

Another energy pulse comes from central London, close to where I stand. Another from a place not far to the north and east, just off the coast. I read the label: Shingle island.

I look again at Doonwreath.

What is curious is that the energy seems to rise above the map, from each point, in all countries, and join together into a huge force field which moves towards me as I stand.

I bend down just in time.

In another moment I would have been destroyed.

I see on the far blank wall the energy path continue on-wards as if into the outer universe, which now seems behind me. Indeed when I look again, I am looking up into the night sky, lit, from moment to moment, by beams of light searching for cascading bombs.

The sirens are constant. Perhaps this is where the next battle will be fought. The last of all.

I move closer to the map. I memorise the locations, from where the most powerful energy comes, the Island and Doonwreath.

Beside them is a smaller version of the familiar symbol.

"I'm glad you came," says a voice behind me.

I jump, then turn. In front of me stands a man, looking at a slight angle, holding a cigar.

He is dressed in a blue boiler suit, and seems to be chuckling.

"You shocked me, Sir! I thought you were a ghost."

"I wish I were a ghost. Come," the man says. "One day we'll go there."

"Where?" I ask.

"There."

The man pauses, before continuing, as if to himself.

"Things grow better in the dark. You thought ours was the last major war. Think again. Learn from me. Then the fight will be for eternity.

Fortunately, though we do not have it, we know where it is."

The man points towards the map of England.

"What?" I ask.

"But so do our enemies."

"What do they know, Sir?"

The man looks at me searchingly.

"The enemy likes to dabble with the Darkness," the man replies. "The enemy has tried to do a deal with .... shall we say, the Other. He has agents everywhere, and will continue to strive until he gets what he wants.

Always. Wherever we go, whatever we do, he will be there, shadowing us, until our will is broken, and then we will be lost. That is why we must not lose. It will be close. But we will win.

Remember, it is always. Deo Concedente."

"I'm sorry. Do you mean, the Spearhead?"

"That, and its successor, which I think you know. No image is for eternity.

Remember this. To fight the enemy we must enter the dark. This war is bad but yours will be worse. It goes to the heart of everything."

"But I don't live in the present!" I say.

The man ignores me.

"We are only vehicles for the gifts we have been given by a higher authority. Mine is to defeat the enemy for now. These bombs that fall on us now will be returned with double force upon the sender until he is crushed. Listen to my speeches. "We will fight on the beaches." I enjoyed that. "We will never surrender." I enjoyed that too. But remember it is the language in conjunction with other instruments that inspire; for words are only a form of symbol too.

Your task is to help to defeat the darkness for the future. But to defeat the enemy, you have to understand him, and to understand him, you have to give up something of yourself, or should I say, become yourself.

For all that's best of dark and light

Meet in the aspect of her eyes.

You see. To fight the dark, you have to enter it, as did Lady Macbeth. Then you will see."

He turns away, and I see a terrifying sight. Where his face had been hangs a dappled mask, his old visage. In its place, a devastating parody of a man, whose life has been lived in darkness, fed by darkness, and almost consumed by it. No features, no integrity, no life.

"Do not be shocked," he says as he faces me again.

"What you see is always a mask. The trained adept learns how to use the right mask to fit the right occasion, while always being truthful to the higher authority, and only for the betterment of the world. Then the enemy can be faced on superior terms.

You had better prepare. The Prime Minister has company, but is expecting you. Be brave. But be careful. Prime Minister's can be tempted too, you know. As can gods. Power is a terrible thing, especially when you are under threat. Watch. Follow what you have been given to do. Do not give in to flattery, or to suspect authority. Help if you can, but your job is too important to stop now, whatever the danger."

"You said the enemy was "him", and then you said, "For all that's best of dark and light/Meet in the aspect of her eyes." "Her" eyes? Why "her"?"

"In order to beat the enemy you have to be very strong. Many fail, and are subsumed, overtaken, corrupted, often by power, but not only power. The Master of the Dark thrives, while the forces of good, dream. Look at the world. But there are times when only action will do."

I repeat my question.

""Her"? It is as the poet said. The oldest, greatest force is feminine. Fortunately the enemy is so vain that he does not see. His time, you see, is limited too. He is afraid to admit of a power greater than his. But the feminine needs help too."

He is silent for a moment, studying me.

"Who did you say you were looking for?"

"The Prime Minister, Sir."

The man chuckles again.

"Oh, yes."

"No. My Prime Minister."

"I will answer your other question but first I have to tell you something else. Burnchester – I have visited it myself, you know – is a sacred site of great power. Our special forces are there now.

What you have experienced there has given you insights into the source. Some of it is in you. Some of it is outside you. It is for you to separate the two. The Darkness – as Macbeth found out, though did not know it; and as Jesus, and other divine teachers, experienced in the wilderness, and did know it – is forever seeking an opportunity to invade, even now. But we must be sure not to call something within, an enemy without. In our case it is clear, but it is not always. I think in yours, it is not clear, except that it is emerging. We must not point the finger of accusation wrongly."

"I don't understand."

I look about me, suddenly anxious. Something is happening to the room.

"I don't have time. I must find my Prime Minister! Please help me. I have something important to say. And then I must go on, I suppose, alone."

I begin to tremble in fear.

The man nods, as if to confirm that things are never completely clear.

Before I move, he points to a staircase leading down below.

"Do not go there, below, unless you have to. Until you are ready."

"But that was just a play. Macbeth is not real."

The man looks at me.

"And Lady Macbeth?"

I turn away angrily. I was in the tunnels, wasn't I? Taken, under the sea! I start up the stairs, hearing the word "goodbye" behind me.

When I turn there is no-one there. The place has completely changed.

I whisper, "goodbye."

*

I push the door and enter a wide chamber.

To my right is the Prime Minister's office. Inside are various screens.

One shows the outside of Burnchester.

Another, Parliament in session.

On a third, a reporter is speaking from a historic site somewhere in China.

There is a second office to the right.

To my left I see the words "Cabinet Room", beside which is a staircase.

Sitting in a small reception area are two military personnel.

One, I recognise as Mr Brock, who had been at the debriefings over the summer. The other I do not know.

Through a nearby window, I notice a police marksman on the roof opposite.

The Cabinet Room door opens and two people exit. It is the emptiness of their stare which gives them away. Anyone who has encountered evil, knows how it drains the breath from life.

One is the Stranger, the other Mr Strangelblood.

I turn away as they pass.

I knock on the Cabinet Room door, and enter.

*

The Prime Minister is with an adviser and three others: the Head of the Security Service, MI5; the Head of the Secret Intelligence Service, MI6, and the Head of the Joint Chiefs of Staff.

They all ignore me.

As the government is under pressure, the adviser explains, the Prime Minister should pre-empt calls for his resignation by offering to resign, whilst warning the House, when he returns shortly, that the consequence would be chaos.

He should say that the country's best hope is to form a government of national unity with him at its Head.

The Prime Minister turns to his security chiefs for an assessment of their recent meeting.

The Head of MI5 confirms that Mr Strangelblood is suspected of being involved in events at Burnchester and possibly Shingle Island, though this has not been confirmed. He has extensive links to organised crime.

He also sponsors research into dark energy, and is an occultist of the most sophisticated, if dubious, kind.

Nevertheless, his offer of help has to be considered. His claim to have the Spearhead under his control would need verifying, but for its power to be at the Prime Minister's disposal would be an advantage.

With regard to Borlick – aka as the Stranger – he and Mr Strangelblood are only temporarily working together, in order to enhance their power.

Before she can continue, I interrupt by introducing myself as an observer from the Burnchester area, with an important message.

As there was nobody to whom I would trust my story, I decided to take it to the top. This minor piece of flattery worked a little.

Despite their surprise, they ask me to continue.

I explain that a relative of mine worked at the Shingle Island base and had escaped by boat last week and told me about the invasion.

She told me that Mr Strangelblood had been present. Not only had he been seen during the battle that destroyed our forces, but seemed to be running the show. The man known as the Stranger, was there also.

My relative had managed to escape just before the place was "sealed-off" by the enemy.

My story confirmed my audience's suspicions. It corresponded with other reports. They didn't ask my identity.

I went on to speak of the Priory's attempts at break-ins at Burnchester, of the information supposedly hidden there, and of the discovery of the parchment.

I told them of the treachery within the school, and of the events there before the school had fallen, and of the emergence of the Dark Figure.

I told them that I had learned, over the years, a little about the secret activities beneath the school, of the visit of military personnel and my attempts to go there myself.

I referred to the murder of the Bishop, and of the main suspects.

The Prime Minister, despite initial doubts, listened more and more carefully as my tale progressed.

He was looking into the abyss, and any intelligence that might offer a way out of his difficulties, had to be considered.

If he was forced to deal with the Stranger and Mr Strangelblood, the more he knew, the better his negotiating position would be. Their claim to have the power to halt the enemy (I supposed through the Spearhead) had to be considered, but they would want guarantees, and a deal.

My worry was that I would be part of it. I began to feel trapped.

The Intelligence Chiefs noted carefully everything I said. My story was not a surprise to them. Mr Rummage – according to Jess, whose father had told her – was thought to have close connections to the intelligence world. Whether he was directly involved, I was not sure.

They would know something of Mr Rummage's activities, as the MOD did; having worked with him on mapping the underground tunnels.

However, I felt sure that Mr Rummage was also working independently, which is why I chose not to disclose everything.

I noticed that the Head of MI5 wore a medallion about her neck, similar to the one my aunt had given me.

I ended by saying, as forcefully as I could, that the Stranger and Mr Strangelblood were traitors, and had to be stopped.

I did not mention the cell.

They asked me why I was telling them this, and what I wanted.

I replied that I wanted the freedom to walk away, and continue my journey. But that I had to warn them. That Mr Strangelblood and the Stranger would try to get them to stop me.

By allowing them to follow me, as they would certainly do,

they had a better chance of finding out what they were really up to. A proper assault could then be planned. And it would buy time.

There were several questions, mostly of detail from the intelligence people: what did I know about the climbing irons on the Church of St Mary Magdalene? Had I seen or heard of the whereabouts of PC Relish, or Mr Gatherin, or M. Le Petit? What did I know about the supposed ability of the Priory to appear and disappear at will? How did I account for the wall around Burnchester and Shingle Island? What did I know of Mr Rummage's research at Burnchester?

To these questions I was evasive.

I think they believed me because of my minor connection with Burnchester. I made sure that my reports were second, if not third, hand.

I told them that Mr Rummage was rumoured to be seeking the source of great power, not just of the Spearhead.

That it involved others including Mr Baxter and Ms Peverell, Dennis and Mrs Wander, her daughter and some of her friends.

"And what are their names?" one of them asked.

"Tyro, Jess, Rick and Tom," I replied.

They asked me what role they had.

I said that, as far as I knew, they were simply a group of friends, and had made discoveries in the grounds, though I did not know what these were or where they were now. I added, perhaps foolishly, that I believed Mr Rummage to have confided in them.

The Head of the Intelligence Service asked me if I had heard that Tyro had left the Dome with an object or anything unusual. She told me to think carefully.

She asked me where I had got my medallion. Then her questions ceased. I was surprised she asked nothing about myself. Perhaps she already knew.

After a brief pause, I asked if I could leave.

144

Before they could answer, there was a loud knock on the door and two people came in.

The atmosphere completely changed. The curious warmth, even intimacy, was replaced by barren, searching cold.

The Prime Minister's adviser spoke.

"Our business is finished, Mr Strangelblood, Mr Borlick. We have nothing further to add to our earlier meeting. Please leave."

I tried to hide my anxiety and looked at the lady. She sensed something and came over to me. She looked into my eyes, as if transferring some secret knowledge. She then walked towards the door at the back of the room, glancing at the two figures.

The Prime Minister got up and made for the door as a cleric, perhaps an archbishop, entered.

Mr Strangelblood spoke. His tone was incisive and clinical. He pointed at me, though I did not look up.

"This person, Prime Minister, is the one we were telling you about. Her name is Tyro. Do not be taken in by her disguise. An art we have perfected, though I say it myself. Those with the gift can change almost at will. Even over time. No doubt she is being controlled by someone else.

She is the carrier of the Object of Power, Prime Minister. The object we mentioned. If she hands over the object, now, we.... er.... might be able to reach an agreement. Save you, in fact, Prime Minister."

He seemed to wave a hand in the direction of the street.

The Prime Minister glanced at his adviser, who answered.

"Agreement Mr Strangelblood, or blackmail? It may work in your business but not with distinguished leaders of nations. I repeat my request, or I shall be forced to call security."

Mr Strangelblood let out a piercing laugh.

Outside, police and the military are filing along Downing Street. The journalists watch, bewildered.

In the doorways stand cloaked figures: silent, deathlike. They move forward.

The Police and military suddenly stop, unable to move.

The journalists freeze.

The Head of MI6, who has been watching through the window, goes over and whispers to the Prime Minister and the Archbishop. Their faces go rigid. Then he addresses Mr Strangelblood and Mr Borlick.

"The conditions, Prime Minister, should be these: that Mr Borlick destroys and shows evidence of the destruction of the parchment that he and the Priory have taken; that he signs a statement to renounce the truth of any of its contents, should, Heaven forbid, there be another copy. If there were, it would be a disaster for the Church, Prime Minister, and for your.... er.... credibility. Most importantly, Mr Strangelblood should immediately call off his forces."

He types a message into his communications system, and hurries out.

The head of Downing Street security enters and confirms that the entire area is surrounded – from Number 10, to the Ministry of Defence, to Parliament and the Great Abbey Church of St Peter. The whole area is in the control of the enemy. As far as he can see, nothing can enter or exit.

The Prime Minister moves towards the window. He wonders what contingency plans are in place for their escape.

He turns to the visitors, pointing to the figures in the street.

"Yours, Mr Strangelblood?"

Mr Strangelblood doesn't react.

The head of the SIS has returned, having tried to establish the security situation elsewhere in the country. There is a communication black-out.

The Archbishop holds the cross about his neck, towards the forces of the dark.

I am close to the back door. I hold on to the cell, beginning to focus all my energies onto it, as I did outside the cafe.

Mr Strangeblood looks directly at the Prime Minister. He speaks without feeling.

"We will hold off our forces, if you give us the girl. Burnchester, Shingle Island and other sites are ours. Soon we will reach Doonwreath. She carries the information and the object that will lead us to our ultimate goal.

We will restore your authority for the short term. Everything will appear normal until we have the final piece in the jigsaw. You might even become a hero. Appear to defeat the enemy and all that. We can make it look as good as you need – for now."

"And your ultimate goal is?"

"Eternity, Prime Minister."

The Prime Minister stands motionless.

My medallion seems to draw in an energy I cannot see. My head begins to spin. I concentrate as hard as I can. I hold the cell.

"There is one other thing. Please tell your intelligence people that we want details of the secret mission being undertaken by Mr Rummage. We are close to unravelling it, but it would save us time. Once we have this we can prevent you and your kind from going into the future, without our, shall we say, guidance. A clever man, Mr Rummage, but misguided."

The Prime Minister glances at his security team. What is Mr Strangeblood referring to? Why hasn't he been told?

His anger is evident, but the situation too critical.

Perhaps the security people don't know either. Mr Rummage may be working alone, or with only those of his choosing.

I look at the faces in front of me.

I take the cell from my pocket, in my enclosed hand. Suddenly I am holding a Spear, the cell its head. An overwhelming energy burns out of it in all directions, seeming to freeze everyone in its compass.

My hand, arm, and body shake, as I try desperately to hold on.

I twist the door handle with my other hand. Everyone in front of me is still.

I turn and see, through the haze, the stairs that will lead me back to the rooms below and I hope into the air.

Outside every person, every figure, is still. For how long I do not know.

Mr Rummage made it clear that the cell would only fully come into its own when it had reached its proper home, and I still did not know where that was. I knew that I had to get to the Island, and trust to fate.

I had to escape. It was my, our, only chance.

I must leave now.

*

Not far from Tyro, in the cover of the park, three figures stand and watch.

They seem to have materialised out of the earth, perhaps the Abbey Church, or even the trunks of the trees, so subtly integrated are they with their surroundings, so barely visible. They are there and not there, according to perception, angle, light. Sometimes they might appear harmless, even protective; at others, as now, their gaze reveals their intention: they will take Tyro and the object that she carries. They will follow her wherever she goes, until she gives up what they claim is theirs.

Tyro reaches the Mall. To her left, the Palace gates are closing. It is too far to see the guards.

Tyro crosses the Mall and walks up the steps towards Waterloo Place. Rompy is nervous.

The three shapes are close by.

Just as she is about to pass, Tyro sees a figure. Before she can avoid it, it brushes past her, knocking her sideways.

She stumbles, regains her balance and continues on, too frightened to look at the darkening outline of the shape, let alone attempt a challenge.

The figure seems to glance round, as if to check whether sufficient contact has been made; as if to check that it has not disturbed her too much. It walks back silently, towards the other two.

Tyro increases her pace, more watchful, but more determined than ever, to reach her goal.

A new energy comes to her. She knows what she must do. There had been a strange peace as she had walked and dreamed. Dreamed of delaying her departure until she had found Jules. Of avoiding the final exit from the city and its inhabitants, who she is beginning to love.

The locations of the Island and Doonwreath are imprinted on her memory. She will head there. Perhaps for the final battle to begin.

She must leave the city, and leave it now.

The watching figures sense her change.

Keeping at a distance, beneath the dark exterior of their robes, their muscles tense, ready for pursuit, ready to take Tyro and the Sacred Cell. But the second attack will be subtle, and out of sight.

\*

Tyro walks hurriedly up Lower Regent Street and into Piccadilly, sensing more shadows on either side, yet she keeps her head straight, flicking her eyes occasionally, as if looking at the traffic, checking to see if they are still there.

Lente, lente currite noctis equi

# Appendix to chapter 10

Extract from a diary written by the Head of SIS and marked, "For the personal attention of the Head of the Security Service." On it is written in a handwritten scrawl: "Top Secret, of course! Speculative! Let me know what you think!"

"Nevertheless there were common features, a pattern. Each incident had taken place around an ancient historic or sacred site, and at each site, the specific building, shrine or temple, or holy place had been transformed in some way. Where images and symbols enriched the inner sanctum, these had been erased, or been changed, so that it would not have been possible to know, from the iconography, after the attacks, to which tradition, historic or holy, the place had belonged.

Locally, many of these events were blamed on groups hostile to the traditions of the site in question. Minorities took the greatest level of blame. Religious sects, racial or ethnic groupings became easy targets for the "sorcery" involved. Though many of the sites represented part of the cultural continuum from which the current status quo had arisen, the acts were seen to be heretical throwbacks, attempts to reinstate some glorious perceived past that most people recognised had never existed.

There was confusion, anger and fear. Accusations were made at anybody who was, had been, or was thought to constitute, a threat. Terrorists, revolutionaries, anarchists, other religions, were all blamed, many people were rounded up.

It was like a new, global reformation.

There was also shame and disbelief that such things could happen on "their" watch (them being the government), with so little ability to control events, or explain them. It was as if some form of social heresy was at work, gnawing at the perceived foundations of the societies concerned, threatening destruction of all that was believed.

Sometimes this sense of inadequacy led to overcompensation, leading governments to claim solutions. This led to the inevitable oversimplifications that are sometimes believed to be needed in order to take action in the world.

The most sophisticated authorities sought explanations – often privately – from whatever source it was thought might supply them. Esoteric groups, academics, keepers of secrets long lost and presumed dead, took on a new potential significance as if they might be able to explain (as if by magic), synchronous events that appeared to be random. Psychologists, alchemists, seers, mystics, psychics, various ancient chivalric and religious orders were covertly targeted for advice, though it was not always easy to penetrate the most ancient traditions, so sophisticated are they at parrying unwanted enquiry. Privately many of these felt a sense of rebirth, not of their particular traditions, but in that, what was emerging beneath the surface, was a collective quest by humanity, manifest as it would be in varying forms, by individuals as much as groups, for a renewed search for a universal Grail.

This awareness may have underpinned the feeling that the secrets at Burnchester were indeed of global significance, though not simply in a direct causal sense, more akin to a talisman, with potential application everywhere.

The above circumstances led to the threat of reprisals and

increased state countermeasures, in a spiral of counterproductive activity which increased the threat of chaos, but was excused in the name of coherence and security.

The situation therefore nominally became worse, not better, in the direst mix of religion, politics, ignorance and the threat of the loss of power, where symbols of state and tradition embodied in places of worship, or cultural significance, even pilgrimage, were concerned. After all, the state survives on legitimate belief, and belief comes in part from the justification of the ethic from which it has grown, and often linked to a philosophy or a religion, explicit or not.

Few, if any, understood the connection of these movements across the world.

*

There were other similarities:

Cloaked figures had been present at each site, though their identity, even existence, was not always proven or clear, and their specific manifestation was not the same in each case. This increased people's sense of a supranatural dimension, enhanced by the talk of the Dark Master, and other archetypal masters of evil. There had been a momentous stand-off between the "attackers" and the defenders. There were often climbing irons.

In most cases the local defence forces had been unable to penetrate the wall surrounding the incident – not even using the most powerful and sophisticated weaponry. It was as if, despite all the best efforts of the guardians of tradition, some other dialogue was taking place, between forces older than time, to which it was possible only to bear witness, and probably misinterpret!

The Americans, the Russians, the Indians and the Chinese, among others, watched events with particular concern. Their vast territories, and interests were potentially, if indirectly, at this stage, under threat. Unknown power is never accept-able to a state's defence apparatus. Incidents become en-meshed in international politics, heightening the already fragile dynamics between governments. There is always a tendency to project the problem onto another state, heighten-ing tension, though it was understood that something "other" was at work, something which threatened the status of humankind. There was increased talk of war."

Added later:

"Security Services monitored events as closely as possible and sought to consult with each other; in that stand-off of mis-trust that forms the bedrock of the instability between the factions in the kaleidoscope of global power. In the private fora in which they operate, they did their best to play down their ignorance, and present each other as if their intelligence was better than it was. So the global confusion increased.

Add the ubiquitous compulsion of the media to dramatise, inflate, extrapolate, mislead, even entertain – not without encouragement and complicity from the consumer and the state – it is not surprising that those who had responsibility for taking action, felt a little inadequate, and those at the receiving end, a little angry.

For once their ignorance was as profound as it was mis-represented, though people's mistrust increased, as a result of years of mismanagement and misinformation, on a mon-strous scale.

Thus, the entire collectivity of global resource: human, tech-nical, military and scientific, was on full alert. Governments were unable to offer any solutions. Every listening device, every observation satellite, the various space stations circling the planet, the complex system of global eavesdropping, sniff-ing, snooping and unravelling, were unable to detect a cause, let alone explain, what was going on."

# 11

MY STORY: THE SEA

Memories come back to me of our joy after leaving Southwold harbour, and of our journey by sea. Jess, Rick and me, with Rompy watching the waves.

Whether we reached our journey's end or not, mattered less than our freedom. Freedom from the terrors of the Dome. And we were together again.

Jess reminded us of the basic instructions, given to us by Mr Rummage.

We were to sail over the submerged city of Dunemoor, then go on to Shingle Island to the north. From there we should begin a long route to the rocky west coast of Scotland to find the Island.

There were many unknowns: the meaning of the documents that we carried, concerning the Priory, the Energies, and the Spearhead, and especially Rick's map of the "stars". These, and the object that I carried, put us at great risk. The figures were not far behind.

Shortly after leaving Southwold, we were sailing over the site of the ancient city. The legendary city I had read about, lost beneath the waves. To the south were the cliffs we had descended that day last summer in pursuit of the figures. A short distance out to sea, their boat the Neptune had lain, from which the figures vanished.

Our boat had a glass panel in the hull. Through it we caught glimpses of the obscure ruins on the sea bed, trailing with weed and embedded in stones and sand. We tried to make out houses and churches – in particular the church of the Knights Templar – close to which the object, reported by PC Relish, was thought to have lain. But before long the turbulent water blurred our view. Our sonar camera made a poor map of the site in consequence.

In the late afternoon, Jess and I turned our attention to unpacking our bags in a space at the entrance of the hold, while the boat swayed and dipped. We were soon absorbed.

During this, Jess told me the story of how she and Rick had escaped. After my desperate flight, the angry figures tried to take them hostage, but they fled to the library and then made their way through the secret door to the tunnels. They followed the path until they found the stream where the boat, which we had seen earlier, was still tied to the landing wall.

In it they paddled downstream until it emerged into the North Sea, at the base of Dunemoor cliff. The route was clearly in use, by whom we did not know.

They saw me on the beach and picked me up.

I wanted to know what had happened to my mum, Dennis and Jess's parents, but all they knew was that they were still fighting the figures as they left.

We unpacked our sleeping bags and took out some food, careful to keep both dry, and tried to make the hold as cosy as possible.

It was soon time to relieve Rick. The sun was setting and the wind had dropped. We were at a standstill.

To our surprise, Rick was looking fixedly out to sea and the tiller was swaying. He didn't even turn when I tapped his shoulder.

Then we realised why.

There in front of us, we saw, not open water as we had

expected, with the shore in the near distance, but a city. A medieval city.

Unwittingly, Rick had stopped, anchored no less, just inside the two piers of the old port, a few hundred yards from the quay wall. There ahead of us, was an entire city, alive!

Boats were being loaded and unloaded by the dockmen. There were fishing vessels and merchantmen. Sailors moved back and forth. Officials observed, recorded, probed. Owners and tradesmen watched anxiously for expected goods. Soldiers stood guard.

We could hear the general noise and hubbub of the port.

We turned to each other, bewildered, excited, nervous. We dare not speak in case the vision passed! Could it be real? I whispered to the others to look for anything that might help us with our mystery. It was bound to be important and we must not miss the signs. Rompy tried to bark, but was too excited!

We couldn't know that we were being observed.

By the quay a larger boat stood in a dry dock, suspended by wooden cranes. Workmen were hammering and sawing, testing and replacing timbers.

There was music from a fair just behind the waterfront. A group of players were performing outside a tavern in the evening light. I noticed a man in a long robe walking towards them, carrying an easel and brushes. There were men and women at gaming tables. There were clerics everywhere. Several church towers rose towards the sky, one rounded like a Temple Dome. I pointed to it. We could just make out its entrance, down a lane.

I tried to think what date this was, but we were too far away to tell.

I suspected it was before Shakespeare's time, judging by the sizes of the ships, though he was reputed to have visited Dunemoor in 1610. Perhaps it was the 14th Century, close to the time when the painting in the Church of St Mary Magdalene was supposed to have been completed.

Mr Baxter once told us that Shakespeare's father had visited Burnchester, possibly with his famous son. I thought of the manuscript we had found in the library, in that "Shakespearean" hand, a copy of which we had. I thought of the players who had danced beneath the veil of the Dome. Who had been in the Burnchester Arms. What would Shakespeare have thought of our tale?

Sailors were drinking outside other taverns along the harbour.

Further on, was a busy market for fish (we could see); spices, wine, dried fruits (I imagined), and further along, woven cloth and garments.

At a separate stall, guarded by two heavily clad soldiers in long robes, was a lady selling jewels. For the first time since the previous summer, I was able to zoom in with my eyes and see what was there. There seemed to be many types of personal ornament: clips, bracelets, necklaces, buckles. There was one special piece which she would not sell to an argumentative friar. It looked like a multi-coloured medallion.

There were townspeople everywhere, watched by soldiers and priests.

To my surprise, we could hear people's conversations both in the market and at the fair, and the chanting of the monks.

On either side of town, which stood on a rise above the harbour, gorse and heather-topped cliffs sank down to lightly hewn sandy fields.

We watched the whole scene, completely enthralled.

Our eyes were drawn to another of the ships at anchor.

Jess turned to me. Rick's eyes broadened. I gasped.

On the side of the hull was an insignia.

The same symbol that we had seen on the ground by Mr Gruff. The same that we had seen on the prow of the

Neptune. There was no doubt about it. The insignia of the Priory.

Yet this was a scene from centuries ago.

*

The image of the Stranger and of the hooded figures on that moonlit night, came to mind, as did the tragic entombing of Burnchester by the evil force the night of my escape.

I recalled the emergence of the Dark Master in the Domed Chamber. I clutched my pocket and felt for the cell. I felt his presence now.

*

I studied the sailors on board this huge ship. Were they able to see us, I wondered, over the centuries?

There were a number of figures in long robes. Many had sword-crosses imaged on their backs. Our fears were confirmed.

"The Knights Templar," Rick said.

*

The Stranger could appear and disappear, seemingly at will. Many of his allies, we were told, were from another time.

Time and no time were here fused.

The words came back to me.

"But 'tis strange;

And often times, to win us to our harm,

The instruments of Darkness tell us truths."

But this was beautiful, not dark. Yet dark was here too.

I thought of Tom, and what he had done to repel the forces arraigned against him. There was a connection I could not fathom. Something emerging in my thoughts of him. "There are many ways to fly," he had said. Perhaps one of these ways was not just across space, which we had all three experienced, but across time as well. Was this one of the weapons the enemy wished to possess?

*

As we watched, the Templar ship set sail.

An ancient bell sounded, from what I was sure was the Templar church.

A crowd had gathered on the quayside to see it go. I imagined some of them to be the Templedeans of Burnchester.

The ship passed close by us.

Some of the figures looked in our direction, but seemed to look through us. Many were dressed for a long campaign.

The strange beauty of the sight was offset by the intense feeling of repressed power that seemed to emerge from another quarter of the town, from where we heard screams, as of prisoners under torture, enemies of the state and church no doubt, privy to something that neither wished to acknowledge: belief in something other than the fodder they had been given through the channels of the known, or presumed.

Other, smaller boats, passed us, following the ship out of the harbour.

We saw soldiers along the coast, as if on alert, preparing for war. I wished we could have travelled inland to see what was happening there. I wished I could tell exactly what year it was. Perhaps Burnchester was even now being built.

*

I wondered if I could travel there in my mind and see the old Dome exposed to the sky, surrounded by ancient stones, hailing oblivion as a memory above, lost amid the heavens of

159

their past, drowned in the orthodoxy of now, and enclosed minds, before they became submerged by the new, and were no longer a reliable experience of eternity.

I decided, as I stood in our small craft, looking out, that I would try to visit Burnchester in my dreams, try to recapture that moment when, after swallowing the potion, I had begun to fly above the grounds in pursuit of the figures.

If I failed, I would continue the training in my own way, until I could reach any place in the world of my choosing, if not at any time of my choosing, for, as I was learning, the moment must always be right. Deo Concedente.

*

All of a sudden, the whole scene disappeared, and we stood looking at the empty sea.

We were dumbstruck and could not talk about what we had seen, for some hours.

*

When night fell, Jess and I slept as best we could in the hold, while Rick kept first watch.

At about midnight he woke us to say that he had seen a shape high in the sky like a mountain range, amid the stars. A cloud passed and it had gone.

I didn't believe him, but later, when I took over, I was proved wrong. In the very early hours of the morning, while Jess was sound asleep, I searched the sky again and there it was. Rick lay on the bottom of the boat, tired out and quiet but not asleep. I apologised to him.

I continued to look up, until my eyes grew tired. The shape disappeared.

I admired Rick for having grown in a way that I was envious of, for I didn't think I had any talents at all, except that

I was the bearer of the cell, which seemed so insignificant, something I could never quite believe.

Rick never flinched from danger, and was always motivated to go on, driven I think by the memory of his friend Tom, whom he missed greatly, though he never spoke about him.

Just before dawn began, another ship appeared on the horizon.

It was a large ship with black sails, visible even in the early light. It was heavily armed with what looked like cannon on either side, peering with dragon-like heads from the chambers of the boat's soul.

It sailed silently and effortlessly.

A priest stood on the prow, conducting what seemed to be a service as the ship approached the quay. A murmur of chanting arose from within.

A large crowd was there to meet her.

When she had tied up, cranes were moved into place and, gradually, huge sacks and wooden caskets were brought up and placed in waiting carts, many driven by superb steeds, controlled by armed horsemen.

After some time, a smaller casket was brought forth, covered in a beautiful silk of red, with lit candles all around it, flickering in the uncertain light. This was carried ashore by six monk-like bearers, who paused on the quay while the Bishop blessed it. The builder of Burnchester Hall stood close by.

There was a long silent vigil, before another service began, and all who were present bowed before the casket, and stayed kneeling for an hour.

Music and incantation filled the air. The whole town seemed to arrive from the quiet side streets, except for the tortured heretic voices lying in the dungeons out of view, confirmed by the trail of blood from their agonising cries.

There were ritual dances of spell-binding power.

161

The full moon struggled in her triple-faced glory with the morning light. Sparks seemed to fill the air. Nothing could enter this sacred space, no earthly power intrude on the moment of its homecoming, whatever this thing was.

The casket was led away to more singing, step by step through the streets, to a dark vault under the crypt of one of the churches in the town. There it was laid, surrounded by a guard of great strength, and other rings of security, and ritual, that kept all onlookers at bay, though every member of the town was allowed to look at the casket once, before it was sealed in its faithfully prepared ground and sunk deep, deep into the earth, into the tunnel that had been chosen for this purpose; for she would, it was hoped, never move again. It seemed like an offering to the Craftsman Image Maker, interred as a sacrifice to the Eternal Power.

During this curious scene, the cell I briefly held, warmed.

At first we wondered what the casket might contain – perhaps the bones of a great warrior, saint or king – but we suspected it could only be one thing.

Our suspicions were confirmed by two crew members from a nearby craft. It was indeed, an object of great devotion. Some called it the Spearhead, others the Sword of Destiny. The Spearhead which had drained blood from the body of a Sacred King. Brought from a secret place in the mountains of southern France.

The great ship left with some new crew and several smaller craft escorting her. As it passed by us, we could see heavily armed, cloaked figures, many with cross-swords on their backs, along the prow and stern. We watched them carefully.

One of the figures looked at me as if he would find me out, even if he could not recognise me. It was as if I was looking into my destiny.

We wanted to talk but, again, could not. The energy that had held us silently, now made us drowsy.

162

We lost control of our senses, and were soon asleep, in the soft sea air, tired from the night's strangeness, as in a dream.

*

The next morning the sky was clear, the sea bare.

We could just make out cliffs to port, but they were not the same. We had sailed north.

There was a beautiful sunrise.

We breakfasted on biscuits and cold tea, which restored our spirits.

Rick took the tiller.

The occasional marker buoy flashed in the morning haze, half-asleep on the surface, like a dreaming fish.

The cliffs went out of sight.

The wind was cool and the sea spray icy.

Later, I took the tiller from Rick. Jess navigated, tracking our progress from snatches of shoreline, and using the compass that Mr Rummage had given us.

Looking back, I can see that Jess was very brave, for she was not an adventurer by nature. I wished I had been less intolerant of her.

Rick was very happy. He would look at Jess and she would ask if he was OK. I said nothing but I knew.

We began to sing, in time with the rolling waves.

When the sun was at its highest, shingle strands began to appear.

In the afternoon, with Rick at the tiller, Jess and I found an odd-looking instrument in the bag given to us by Mr Rummage. It was composed of interconnected circular metal rings with planet-like objects suspended between them. The pieces seemed to move, making it feel alive. We put it aside, as we were hungry.

"Scary, isn't it?" Jess said, unwrapping some food.

163

"What? This thing?"

"All because of the picnic we never had!"

"You mean last night?"

She didn't answer. I could see she was trying to think of a response.

"What is this thing?" I asked, picking the object up, carefully.

She said that it was a sort of astrolabe. A beautiful instrument that shows the movement of the planets relative to the sun and earth. Her father had one, and had showed her how it worked. If you moved one element, everything else moved in relation to it. I found it curious, like the inner working of a sea creature, perhaps a lobster, or crab.

"Will it help us find our way?"

"Maybe, with someone's help. It's more for astronomy than for navigation. We need a sextant. Anyway, one of the planet things seems to be missing."

"Mr Rummage must have had a reason."

It seemed a strange thing to include in our things, the more so because it was old and incomplete, though otherwise in good condition.

"About last night. How.... I mean what....?"

"It was weird, Ty. I don't know. What do you think?"

It wasn't often Jess asked me anything. I looked at the sea.

"Perhaps we can see into the past," I said, trying not to seem foolish. "I was thinking about what Tom said. It seems to fit."

"We seemed to be in the present, though. Perhaps the past is always present, if we choose to see it."

"Or becomes visible only at certain times," Rick called. I didn't realise he had been listening.

"To some people...."

"Who choose to look."

"Or to whom it appears."

The subject was dropped. I think because we didn't really know.

We were sailing at some speed now.

I lowered my voice.

"But why us?"

"I'm sure plenty of people would have seen it," Jess said in her thoughtful way, "but only we have been given the chance. For that reason we have to continue."

Jess handed Rick a sandwich.

I asked her what she thought the cell was. She said that she hadn't really studied it. So I took it out of its case and placed it in the bottom of the boat.

It lay beside the astrolabe (which Jess decided should be called an Armilla, so we christened it an astrometer, which sort of rhymed), like a star out of its orbit. The astrometer had become smaller, so much so, that we would have no difficulty in carrying it now.

Jess picked the cell up and looked at it carefully, the afternoon sunlight reflecting off its surface.

"I don't suppose anybody knows what it is," she said, "let alone realises the power it has."

At first it seemed like a small arrowhead. Then it appeared in the shape of a heart. It reflected different coloured lights.

"We don't know that it has, do we? All we know is how we came by it."

"I know it has power. I can feel it. Besides, why else would the Stranger and his crew want it? Why else would we be hunted day and night, over land and sea, even over time, for a "nothing". They – the figures – know it is special. It might even be the Grail – in disguise. Remember who gave it to us. It must be something to do with the casket that arrived last night."

"What do you mean?"

"Think about it. The Grail seems to be visible only at certain times, and to certain people. Also, it hasn't always been spoken about in such a mystical way. Perhaps it changes

165

shape, or should I say we change it, somehow, to fit in with circumstances?"

"You mean that the Grail only exists in our imaginations. And so it is our imaginations which give it shape."

"Who controls our imaginations? The Reverend Sandals wasn't sure even that it exists."

"Or that people weren't looking in the right place."

"It seems that the images and symbols that are important to us, change over time. Look at all the old gods we no longer worship."

"Why do you think the figure in the painting disappeared?"

"Perhaps the image is no longer as important now as it once was, and whoever controls these things, realises it. That is why we must find the Image Maker. The source of the images we worship. He or she must be working on something new. The old images are tired, don't you think?"

"Like me! The Image Maker must make things for a reason."

"Being insignificant is the cell's best protection," I said taking it back. "Maybe it will become something big and important one day."

"I suppose we'll know what to do with it when the time comes. As for power, perhaps it's all a trick."

"You mean, it – the Grail or the cell – is something to believe in, that has the power to draw down and transform, but no power in itself?"

"But that would only work if people knew a bit about it. If there was a story attached to it. A story everyone believed and loved, that gave them strength and purpose, perhaps everlasting life.

I think I'd rather find the Spearhead, the thing that has never been found. At least I'd know it was important, and looked important. I could link it to the painting. But the cell doesn't have a story. There's no human suffering attached to it. Nothing that makes us die and live again."

166

"The Spearhead may not exist either."

"People believe in it. Have killed for it. May kill again. That's real. I'm sure that's what arrived last night."

"People have fought for much less. History is full of people battling over beliefs."

"Perhaps it is up to us to let everybody know that we have the cell and why it's important."

"But we don't know why it's important."

Jess paused before continuing.

"There must be a story. A story that people can believe in."

"We could discover parchments that tell its history."

"I think it's like a seed. But what of I don't know. The way it appeared was very strange."

"Perhaps we should give it a test, or invent a story," I said jokingly.

"You mean like throw it into the sea and see if it comes back to us of its own accord. Walk on water, so to speak. That way we would know that it was meant for us, and we for it, and have power."

"That would be tempting fate. I think it's passed already, given the circumstances."

I was surprised at myself for saying this.

"If we find its proper home – as we're supposed to – that might solve all sorts of problems and allow us to be free from pursuit and danger," Jess said, trying to pick up the cell again.

I held her arm, and shook my head. I felt sure she was testing me. Testing my resolve.

"It can't work if you don't believe in it."

"Believing where we cannot prove," Jess murmured. "We must have faith."

"Not just in anything, though...."

"Why not?

"As you said. There must be a story. There has never been faith without a story. And images to go with it. And truth."

"And martyrs."

We looked up and caught the spray from a large wave that had lashed the prow and rocked the boat. We grabbed the side. The cell didn't move.

"'s not my fault!" Rick yelled, trying to steady.

The gust passed and the boat settled.

"It looks as if the mist's coming down. I don't fancy drifting about with no wind and without being able to see. Especially if there are sand banks. We might run aground, and that would be a disaster."

Jess closed the map as the shoreline was out of sight.

"We might as well study the astrometer!"

We looked at it, as if it might tell us something. Then towards the sky, which was quite invisible. No chance of seeing any shapes now.

"We're in the hands of the elements," Jess said playfully.

She could sense that I wanted to say something. I was anxious, as if there might not be another chance.

I returned to our conversation.

"Do you think that some of the things that happened to us really happened, Jess?"

"You mean the things in the summer – like flying? It seems impossible, yet I can't forget it, and I feel guilty about it. Then there's the DC – remember?"

"I think I was only half-conscious," I continued, as if to re-assure myself. "The image in the painting. The Dome itself. The figures. They must have happened because of the fact that we're here. But I don't know if anyone would believe us."

"The whole world knows all about what happened at Burnchester, so far as they can tell from the outside," said Jess. "And remember the tunnels and the secret chamber below? People know about those. There are lots of pieces that we don't know about. We can do our best though. Somebody must. Let's concentrate on what we have been given to do."

"Something very extraordinary is happening to our world,

something frightening. And we – ordinary us – are at the centre of it! Is it enough to believe?"

"Well, in so far as we have a role like others, and we can only see things really from our own point of view, yes. But it's always best to try to see things also from other people's, I always think."

"You may think I've lost my nerve, Jess, but I'd rather be at home, moaning at mum, and doing, or thinking of doing the washing up, even my homework."

"It's no good thinking like that Ty. It's like your plastic sword. You can't go back. The past can never be retrieved. You have to do what is required of you. That much I have learned."

I thought of my cross-sword. I had thrown it away in a fit of fury in the church at school that day when Vipers had locked us in. I had once wanted it with me, and I thought about it occasionally, still. But its time had passed.

"The past is always with us, Jess, as we have just seen. One day Burnchester and all its mysteries may be under the sea too."

"I think the boat we saw coming into harbour was carrying the Spearhead, and we saw the ceremony of its placement in the crypt of the church, hundreds of years ago."

"You mean like somebody, or something, wanted us to know it had happened, even though we cannot find it now?"

"Maybe."

"And do you think that some of the people saw us looking back at them, as if from the future?"

"Perhaps they could sense the cell, and its importance. A few of them. One or two anyway."

"But you can never tell the importance of the future from the present."

"Of course you can. Otherwise we would never survive, or grow. That is why they have sent out their people to find us. They knew about us even then. They have galloped over time.

That is what the figures are. Timeless things sent into the future to protect their present, and try to return them to a gloried past. If they destroy us we'll all go backwards. If we win, they will die forever."

"So they are after us, in their future, as we can see them in the past?"

"It's not an equation of equal parts. The future is never as predicted, nor the past ever as presumed, and the line between them is twisted and always moving. Like light. Like energy. That is why we must reach our goal, for by going into the future, we discover the past, and then find when we arrive ("as if", in the words of the poet, "for the first time") that it was already there, in another form, though we did not see it."

"You read too much."

We both laughed.

"And understand nothing! Of course, even if we win and the enemy dies, they will come again in another form. The act of creation is eternal, and it requires both light and dark, and has always done so. All we can do is help the balance in the direction of good. But we must not forget the dark. In fact, as you always say, "the Instruments of Darkness tell us truths.

The cell, the thing we have been given is another form of the Grail, but only those living in the past, with the exception of a few magi like Mr Rummage, know it. That is why the Priory have returned, and want it before it takes on a form that they cannot destroy; until they themselves have been transmuted into a new form themselves. They are always slower, that is the joy of making images. They see the threats before we do. Which is why they have survived so long. But we can beat them I am sure, though others will challenge us."

We paused, uncertain of what we had said or even if it was us who had been speaking. It was as if we were speaking in tongues.

"Jess, can you take the tiller? I want to bring the main sail in."

"I wonder," I shouted above the spray. "If we could fly above, why not below, into the deep? What we saw last night may have been real, or an apparition, but there must be something at the bottom of the sea, for us to visit?"

"No magic potion, no oxygen," Jess said, teasingly. "We have to develop...."

"If only we could read the signs and realise that the future is all around us. We'd be rich, as fortune tellers."

"Except that I don't want to be. There'd be no journey either, which is all that matters."

I looked at her.

"What I mean is this: suppose we did know the future. What good would it do? People might pay for the knowledge, but it wouldn't alter it, would it? So we are better off carrying on as we are, muddling from day to day, choosing...."

Jess looked at me, then at the cell, which I picked up. It now seemed unblemished. I put it away.

"Choice is conditional, like everything else, except perhaps love."

The boat began to sway from side to side, as I moved to the jib, which I tightened in the breeze.

"Do you remember what I asked you in the tunnels all those months ago Jess?"

Jess was at the tiller. She must have known what I was going to say: that she had not abandoned me.

Rick began to reef the mainsail.

"At least you've got someone," I said.

Jess lowered her eyes and said nothing. I know Rick heard.

˙ Rick suddenly shouted. He was pointing at what seemed to be a shadow under the water ahead of us.

At first I saw nothing, then, amidst the breaking waves, I saw what looked like a dark moving shape.

Rompy started to bark.

"A shark?" I cried, jokingly.

Jess swung the tiller round and we all lurched forward. Rompy nearly went overboard.

"Jess!"

"Sorry!"

"Where is it?"

"Gone."

We were silent for several seconds, staring at the water.

"Perhaps it was a whale."

"There aren't whales in the North Sea."

"There are, sometimes," I said.

The shape appeared beneath the surface, but it was difficult to see.

When the boat righted it had gone.

I took hold of Rompy, who was still agitated, and tried to calm him.

"It must have been a sandbank," Rick said.

"Sandbanks don't move."

"At least they won't be able to follow us here."

It was the first time since leaving that anyone had mentioned the figures.

"We have no choice but to head for Shingle Island."

\*

How? I wondered. We weren't exactly expert sailors, our boat was little more than a dinghy, and our supplies would run out in a few days. It wasn't clear how far we would get.

As if to avoid the subject further Jess, who had handed the tiller back to Rick, and I, tried to prepare a hot drink, which was difficult in the wind and spray. I was forced to go into the hold and light the small stove. I held the stove, Jess the can of water above it. I thought of the agents during the war who had to survive, often alone, behind enemy lines, and wondered how they managed.

# 12

Later in the afternoon what looked like a stout fishing vessel appeared on the horizon.

For the next couple of hours we had to navigate through the ridges of sand which had become more frequent.

Jess and I had to use the oars to keep us from running aground.

We put our hoods and scarves on, to keep out the cold.

When we reached an area of open sea again, Rick was able to tack, and for a while we made steady progress.

The vessel sailed closer.

She was several times longer than us, and radar and satellite discs suggested a very modern boat, though she looked battered, and we couldn't make out any markings.

When she was twenty metres away, she turned and slowed, almost alongside.

Rick watched the boat carefully, while Jess and I looked out for sandbanks.

Two men emerged from the large cabin.

Rompy barked.

"Do you need any help?" One of the men shouted.

"We're OK, thanks!" Rick answered, cautiously.

"These are treacherous waters. There are some unsavoury characters about."

We could see what looked like gun placements hidden

discreetly under the square stacks on the prow. There were several satellite receptor dishes. The vessel was very high-tech indeed, despite the scruffy outside. I couldn't see a name. The flag seemed like a red ensign, but I wasn't sure.

"Where are you heading?"

The man spoke as if he was holding something back. He had an unusual accent.

"North, if we get through. We don't seem to have much choice."

"And you?" asked Jess, turning.

"The weather's going to change. Watch out for strange vessels."

Rick asked him what sort of vessels.

I wondered if he meant smuggling from the big ports.

"A boat recently sank not far from here, with many people on board. All were drowned."

Perhaps he was trying to scare us off. I thought of our vision of the night before.

"Where did you say you were heading?" Jess asked again.

"Don't stop at Shingle Island. You should sail on to the Great Estuary further along the coast. There are plenty of creeks for you to land on. You should make it before dark. Avoid Shingle Island."

"But we've been given instructions."

There was a pause. Had Rick said the wrong thing? The men were surprised. Then something clicked.

"Who by?"

"Who are you?" Jess asked.

The man didn't answer.

"These are very dangerous times," he said. "The MOD is very jittery, especially after what happened at Burnchester. Everyone is on high alert. Who gave you instructions?"

"Mr Ru....!" Jess stopped Rick short.

It was too late. The man had heard. His tone changed again. He asked us if we had seen any unusual vessels.

"Yes," I said, coming forward.

The man hadn't noticed me.

"Where? When?"

"I'll tell you when you answer my friend's question. We don't give information to strangers."

"Shingle Island is a top secret research station. There has been enemy activity there. You will be in grave danger if you trespass."

The second man said something to his colleague and went below.

"But it is nearly night," Rick said, "and the weather is worsening. We must land soon or we'll perish."

"Sail on as far as you can. I would give you a tow now, but we're under strict instructions to continue our patrol. We cannot afford another breach at Shingle Island."

"Is it serious?" Jess asked.

"Yes. Not least because it was unseen."

The second man returned with a small, tightly sealed case.

He threw it towards us.

The bag went under a few metres from us, and then bobbed up and hung there, like a buoy.

We were cautious.

"It's an emergency communication system. There are also some rations, weather proofing and flares, besides satellite phones, and position devices."

Jess and I pulled it in with one of the oars.

"We know who you are. You never know when you might need them. Our compliments."

When we landed it, Rompy sniffed as if it had been a fish.

We looked at each other.

"Are you from the Special Boat Service....?" Rick asked.

The crack Royal Navy unit that even I had heard of.

Their boat was now a few feet from us. The first man, we assumed the commander, boarded. He was wearing a dry suit, and carried an automatic weapon on his back, and had several other pieces of equipment about him.

He spoke hurriedly.

"What I am about to tell you is between you and me. There has been activity by unidentified forces, above and below the surface, for some time. Who or whatever the enemy is, they are extremely dangerous, and have caused serious damage. They are likely to intrude again.

If you get into difficulty or see anything, call us immediately. We want to know who and what you have seen. You mentioned strangers, unusual vessels."

He was looking at me.

I told him of the figures we had seen at the harbour. I mentioned the boats. He listened with great care, told us again to be very vigilant and to contact him about anything unusual.

He was making a contract, as Mr Rummage used to do.

He then held out his hand.

"I'm Captain Blake. Your father, Tyro, was a great man. Your journey is important to us all. Good luck. Avoid the Island."

I was shocked, but my pulse raced. He shook hands with Jess and Rick.

"Don't identify yourselves. Sorry. Time is short."

We asked him who the enemy were.

He didn't know who or what.

I asked him for any news of Burnchester, but he didn't have any.

"Did you say who or *what* the enemy might be? Are you suggesting that they might come from....?" Rick asked.

The Captain put his hand up. He continued.

"If you see lights in the sky, most will be surveillance helicopters."

Mr Greenshank had mentioned lights in the sky.

"Finally, Tyro, Jess and Rick. You must learn when not to ask questions, at least when not to expect answers."

"Why?" countered Rick. "It's us who are in danger, in unknown waters! Not you. A lot of good you are!"

Rick hadn't reacted like this since he argued with Mr Vespers.

"Knowledge is sometimes power, and with it comes danger. What you carry is dangerous. What the enemy sought at Burnchester was knowledge. I will tell you. Anything – I mean anything – is possible in this changing world of ours. We are entering a new phase of human and other forms of knowledge. The research that is being carried out near here-about which Tyro's father knew – might transform our view of the world."

He paused.

"I've even heard that it is possible, sometimes, to.... fly. Best not to mention it, though. People might destroy you, or want it for themselves. Goodbye."

The Captain turned and re-boarded his vessel.

I liked him despite his way, like the sea wind, of searching us all out. I thought he was unfair to Rick. Jess, surprisingly, told me not to be so critical. I became angry, and reminded her who was carrying the cell. Then I felt guilty because of her loyalty and because of the sacrifices she had made to be here.

Rick quietened us by reminding us that night would soon fall and we were in dangerous waters.

The Captain's boat seemed to lie off at some distance, while we made slow progress. Then it disappeared. A couple of hours later it reappeared on the horizon, moving in and out of sight. It was on a heading north, between us and the shore.

Later they sent up a flare, which made us cheer. It lit the whole seascape in a fantastic glow. The light seemed to hang in the air for some time. Held up for our benefit, as if by some other hand.

Then the boat went out of sight behind a spit of sand. I had a feeling we would never see the Captain again.

Dusk began to fall and the wind increased. The sky grew dense, gulls flew low, and the salty spray strafed us hard as we plunged in and out of the waves.

Rick struggled to keep the tiller steady. Jess bent over the side, clutching her tummy. I went over to her and held her. Her face seemed worn and drained.

The heaving grey waves seemed sad. I wondered how long any of us would survive if we fell overboard.

What was the Captain hinting at? What dangers awaited us? We were not far from the discovery of the object on the sea bed. I thought I saw the ruins of Burnchester Hall beneath the waves, but the image was soon gone. I fell back in tears.

It was at this point that I first saw what looked like jelly fish, but they were larger, silently, slowly making their way, tumbling and turning, just below the surface, towards the shore.

Would our listening devices be enough to detect such things?

I called out.

"Barrels!"

Rick had seen them and struggled to avoid the nearest.

It came to within inches of our bow. There were several others. They would certainly sink us. One had sprung a leak and left a trail of slime in its wake. There was something moving on it that clung to the surface.

We had no idea what it was.

We tried to identify the barrel but it was impossible. We scanned the sea for more.

The wind continued from the south and the sky and the sea became almost one.

We were more tired than we realised.

Jess felt better and gave me a hug, then went over to Rick and gave him a kiss.

They looked a noble pair, older than they were, looking far ahead in the bleak light, hair flowing back in the wind. Jess was lucky. Looking back now, I should have known.

The astrometer had slowed. I looked at it closely. I had the impression that the planet-like shapes, were not the same as they had been before.

*

I took the pack and went inside the hold. At the top I found a knife, a torch, some rations and three smaller bags. The smallest and heaviest was marked "communication". The second contained a tent and sleeping bags. The third had no markings at all.

The wind dropped and we entered a patch of mist. Rick and Jess appeared like statues through the gloom.

I could make out what looked like a shoreline to port.

There were old fence posts a few metres inland.

Lengths of rusted wire fell onto the pebbles, like forgotten spider webs.

We took down the sail and jib and startled to paddle.

"Looks like WW2 defences," Rick whispered.

"Where are we?" asked Jess.

"Shingle Island if I'm not mistaken. Doesn't look top secret to me. Ideal campsite for the night."

I didn't like the feel of the place.

The beach fell away and a watchtower appeared, horribly wind-beaten and skeletal, with a rough lookout shelter twenty metres up.

"Nothing telling us to keep out," Rick said.

"Let's land," I said, "and climb the tower."

"We won't see anything," Jess said.

Rompy sniffed cautiously.

The bottom of the boat scraped the shingle. We jumped out and pulled her ashore.

We looked out over a flat waste, like a hidden desert of stones, but for an old broken-down hut. There was no sign of any security. There was a slight rise ahead of us.

"I don't think much of their defences."

"Maybe it's not Shingle Island."

"We'd better camp anyway."

"I don't like it," said Jess.

I secured the line around an old fence post and helped put up the tent, Jess objecting, but it was two to one.

It had got colder.

We unpacked the food and the communication system that the Captain had given us and placed them with the flares and the GPS close to the entrance.

"Let's light a fire," Rick said, enthusiastically.

"In this wind?"

"What with?"

"What are you whispering for?"

Rompy and I went along the beach one way, to look for drift-wood, while Rick and Jess went the other. It didn't take us long to gather enough for a fire. Rompy picked up a piece of old rope. I found an unusual stone beside it which I put in my pocket.

As we returned to camp, I noticed something in the distance, beyond the shingle rise.

I reached camp, threw the wood down and pointed behind me, unable to speak. Jess gave me a drink of water, while Rick ran to look.

He returned, very excited.

"It's amazing."

"I was trying to tell you," I choked.

"What is it?" Jess asked.

"It's a huge, long building. Like an enormous hangar."

"We'll have to investigate."

"No way! We've had the clearest warning. If this is Shingle Island, we shouldn't even be here," Jess said, angrily.

"We have to!" Rick replied.

"No we don't! Don't be so stupid! We shouldn't even have landed!"

"If we hadn't, we'd have died of cold!"

I managed to calm Jess by saying that Mr Rummage had told us to land, which I thought was more compelling than the Captain's warning.

"Mr Rummage might be dead!"

"Jess!"

"I'm sorry."

We dug a small pit and made a fire.

Jess found the other two pairs of binoculars and gave one to me, the other to Rick.

"We'd better go, before it's completely dark. But I won't go all the way."

Rick and I stared.

"Thanks, Jess!" I said, giving her a big hug.

The three of us and Rompy hurried up the beach, in the oncoming dark.

Part of me wished I hadn't seen the building, when I remembered other nocturnal adventures.

The waves were breaking onto the shore behind us, and drawing back as if in pain. I checked the cell.

We crawled the last few feet to the top. Dusk lowered in the sky, like an explosion afterglow. I whispered to Rompy to sit. He laid his head on the top of the rise and looked over. Blessed Rompy.

I couldn't see anything at first.

Then, I made out a tree against the far horizon. Next to it was a small clump, camouflaging a hut.

I scanned to the right. A wall appeared just above ground level, like a box inside a crumpled sheet.

It became a huge low building, bigger than the largest hanger you've ever seen.

It was several hundred metres long, and appeared almost

as many deep. The shiny wall was the same height all around and seemed to rise out of the shingle. At each end there was a tower with lower towers at regular intervals in between.

"Wow!"

"What on earth?"

"There are no windows or doors."

Nor was there any obvious security.

"See how it blends in with the shingle. Mr Rummage meant us to see it alright. We must be on Shingle Island."

"Why, I wonder?" I said.

The building was very new.

What seemed to be wires arose from the towers.

"There's a whole mass of them, like a huge web."

"They don't all touch though. Some are suspended apart."

The sea wind was augmented by a hum.

We looked at each other.

"Just like the wires in the tunnels at Burnchester."

"Rumbags wouldn't want us not to look at it, I suppose," Jess said, taking hold of my arm. "He must have had a reason."

"We'd better go there now, before it gets too dark," said Rick.

"Or we might miss something important."

If I had known what was later going to happen, I would never have suggested it. Never.

We ran down to camp, and found some food and water for us to take, along with a torch and one of the phones.

Jess said that she would only hold us back, and would look after the camp, but asked us not go out of sight, for her sake. And not be too long.

The fire flared up, as if to remind us of our comforts, as well as the dangers. If our tent, or worse, the boat caught alight, we would be finished.

I gave Jess another hug.

"Thanks," I said.

"Take care. Both of you," she said.

We checked our watches.

"I'll have the camp organised for when you return."

"Thanks," Rick said, running over to her.

Rick and I walked up the bank, and headed over the open ground.

# 13

I tested the phone. Jess responded by saying she was watching us from the hill. I turned round, but could only see the slow gradient of stones, with the odd patch of grass, leading towards the sea.

To my horror, I thought I could see a barrel drifting ashore. I told Jess, but she wasn't worried.

We passed a sign saying "Ministry of Defence: Keep Out." There were others across the shingle. Why hadn't we seen them before?

After a few minutes, the building seemed to hurry towards us. The lower towers were clearly located on the inside of the wall, and it was from these, mainly, that the wires arose.

As we thought, some were not connected, though many did seem to touch. They pointed into the night sky at different angles. One or two moved, and then stopped, like the hands of a disjointed clock.

There was no sign of anybody.

"It's amazing," I said.

"Yeah!"

"But spoooooky."

"Where are the people?"

"Watching us, no doubt."

I didn't find Rick's attempt at a joke very funny.

As we approached the building, we could see a concrete roadway running along the base of the wall. On it was a set of tracks. At intervals of about a hundred metres was a set of lights, each with a different combination of colours. Some flashed on and off, others were static. They seemed orchestrated.

The building lay inside what seemed a massive bomb crater, and was built with great precision, reminding me of a vast computer.

The hum was now overbearing. Powerful enough to drown out our phone. We felt sure we were out of sight of Jess, but were too excited to turn back.

We crossed the track to the wall.

As we did so, a set of lights to our right changed colours.

We looked along the track, then looked up.

There was nothing to climb up, nothing to hold on to. No escape ladders.

Then, to my horror, I noticed a figure standing on the top of one of the towers, watching us. Rick was looking at the wires and didn't notice it. It moved off.

"Rick, there's someone there!"

He didn't seem interested.

"It's too late to go back now. Those wires," he whispered, excitedly. "Remind you of something?"

I couldn't think.

From behind us came a terrible noise.

I grabbed Rick's arm and told him to run. We hid behind the notice-board.

A vehicle, like a curious rectangular container, had stopped on the track beside a set of lights.

On it, transmission aerials pointed upwards. From them beams of energy pulsated into the air.

The sea spray seemed to dissolve into plumes of steam.

Above, now visible for the first time, some sort of sky craft responded from high up, though we could not see it clearly. I was completely bewildered.

Within moments the craft disappeared, and from the back

of the vehicle, a mechanical arm stretched outwards and connected itself to a handle which had appeared on the hangar
wall. It pulled the handle and opened a hidden door.

Without thinking, we ran as fast as we could, jumped the
track at the back of the vehicle, and forced our way through
the opening, pushing past something that seemed to be coming out.

We reached an inner wall beside a stairwell from which a
circular staircase led upwards. We could hear footsteps
descending but could see nothing. Again, we felt something
pushing past us.

Beside the stairwell was a lift. The lights beside the door
were similar to those beneath the library at Burnchester. We
were both shocked and terrified.

The wall door remained open for a few moments. I could
just make out a second vehicle parked behind the first. This
was longer and taller. There were no windows, though there
was an opening at the back. Both vehicles began to move. Our
door then shut and we were locked in.

Rick pointed to the stairs. There was no time for talk. We
had to make the most of the opportunity, and were too afraid
to think of how we were going to get out.

As we climbed, I heard Jess's voice. I raised the phone to
my ear.

"Rick, Ty, where are you? I can't see you! Come quickly.
We're being surrounded! Hurry!"

"Jess. We're inside. What do you mean surrounded? We
don't know how we're going to get out. We'll look out from
the top of the wall, if we can. We're going up now. Did you
see the aircraft thing, and the energy rays?"

"They just appeared from.... oh no! There are more. It's so
weird. It's like they're not people at all. Figures emerging
from the beach, in lines, and now slowly walking towards
you. Come quickly. What shall I do? I'll try to fol.... Help!"

Her voice cut off before I could answer. I imagined Jess

alone, on the cold beach, frightened out of her life. I was angry at myself. The only thing we could do was to go on and try to find another way out.

At the top of the stairs we reached a parapet which followed the length of the building. Standing on our toes we could look over the top. The wind was fierce.

In one direction we could see the ground we had covered, rising gently, then falling towards the sea. Behind the central incline was our camp. We could just make out the top of the boat. Jess was nowhere to be seen.

Inland to the west I could see the hut in the grove of trees. Several vehicles were parked beside it, and there was a boat tied up beyond. This must have been the river side of the island.

The expanse of shingle appeared empty but then they emerged, as if created from the tomb of the earth. Line after line of figures, like those at Burnchester, moving towards us; unidentifiable, dark, unstoppable, like an invading army. They were faceless and cloaked.

All along the beach, both north and south, other figures seemed to emerge; as if from the toxic mixture that poured from the barrels that had been disgorged from the sea. Out of the graves, perhaps, of what we were building for ourselves.

Far out to sea, lay a ship. It was the one that we had seen the previous night leaving the medieval port of Dunemoor.

"The figures! Can you see?" I heard Jess scream. "They're everywhere. Come quickly. They have not seen me yet, nor our tent, hidden as it is. But it is only a matter of time. I'm going to follow you. So look out for me."

"No Jess! Stay where you are! Try to hide. Anywhere! We will come and find you! Stay where you are!" I shouted.

I looked at Rick in desperation.

Along the beach three heavily armed boats came into view, led by a fourth, rather shabbier, but equally fast. It took charge.

"It's Captain Blake!" I shouted.

From all four boats, smaller landing craft took off carrying groups of heavily armed soldiers. These landed and ran ashore, making their way up the beach as fast as they could.

Some moved sideways, others fell to the ground, taking up cover positions, while others went forward, closing behind the figures.

At the same time, across the empty landscape, on roads that were hidden in the shingle, armed vehicles had appeared and rumbled across the waste.

More vehicles seemed to emerge out of the ground, and moved forwards pointing their weapons at the figures. Out of the dimly lit sky, three helicopters came. Sirens sounded everywhere.

The Captain's men took up position.

The figures moved forward, unconcerned. There were repeated calls for them to stop. Laser weapons were fired in warning. More military personnel arrived. Other figures appeared, as if preordained, between the soldiers and our building.

If the soldiers fired in our direction, the site would be damaged. The military could do nothing.

On the figures came. Towards the wall. Towards us. We ran along the parapet searching for an exit, fearing to go back down the way we had come. We had to save Jess.

We could now see inside the wall for the first time.

Below, a vast circular disc faced the sky. Wires were all around us. From these, pulses of energy raced upwards, carrying tiny particles of light.

Outside, the figures were close to the wall, the soldiers closing in on them.

We heard gunfire. Explosions, turmoil.

Then suddenly, everything, inside and out, stopped still.

I turned and stared in disbelief.

The figures stopped, as did the army. All vehicles, all

instructions, all noise ceased. A vast web of antennae seemed to burst out, like an orchestra of light into the atmosphere.

Looking up I could see, it seemed, into the heavens, far beyond our earth. What seemed like a vehicle received the light beams and responded in kind. These were picked up by other antennae in the sunken disc.

The beams of light continued to pulse upwards, wave after wave of energy, from below the earth and up to the sky. Down came the response, received into the vast bowl below.

Rick and I looked down, amazed.

In front of us was the huge circular receiver dish, hundreds of metres across, the nadir deep in the pit.

At the base of the dish was a wire, with an opening beneath it.

The whole dish seemed to float. It rotated a few metres then stopped, and rotated again. When it stopped, an array of transmitter wires at the top edges of the outer circumference emitted powerful beams, though the transmitters changed at each stop. A curious dialogue of energy seemed to take place between the earth transmitters and the sky.

At the top of the inner wall, inside each of the twelve towers, guards stood still in front of carved stones that the towers housed. All had faces like empty masks. The stones looked like spears.

Rick and I ran forward, but there were no exits. We returned to where we had entered but found nothing. We ran forwards again, passing one of the empty, staring faces which looked out over the hollow beneath. A little further on we found an opening.

But instead of leading into another stairwell, and we hoped to the outside, it led inwards towards the centre of the vast parabola.

We had to cross a small gangway, and then slide down the face of the dish.

As far as we could see, between the movement of the huge

shape and the vast energy beaming out and back, the slide led to beneath the central antennae, into the crevice like the mouth of doom.

The moment was decisive.

I looked at Rick and saw his determination. We had to try anything to get out. There had to be some way out beneath this inverted dome.

The vast receiver stopped and in the pause, I walked out onto the gangway.

I stood at the top of the disc and, just as it began to turn again, jumped. I fell onto the shiny surface, but instead of sliding down, I came to an abrupt halt. Steps had emerged out of the sides at my touch, and held me.

When I regained my balance, I started down, Rick following.

As we descended, I looked closely at the shiny sides of the huge disc and then up at the sky.

It was like a vast, circular auditorium. The array of light and energy was fantastic.

We watched the sides of the disc close in on us as we approached the focal point at the base, which seemed to enter below the earth.

The central wire in the base drew closer.

Beneath this was a gap.

The whole disc was suspended above four buttresses – like arches fixed into the earth.

Our stairs led between two of these into the dark below.

There, deep in the abyss, I saw, or thought I saw, as I descended, a half-human shape emerge. Its turbulent eyes were dark. It seemed to struggle upwards, desperate to clutch the crown of light and air that appeared within its grasp.

It tried again and again to ascend out of the slough, but each time was repulsed by the beams of light from above. Finally it fell back, crumpled like a beaten angel, in a dark robe.

I was transfixed, Rick at my side. Was it towards this that we were going?

I had seen the same shape appear in the Domed Chamber at Burnchester that day, on the top of the plinth. Then it had spoken and nearly taken us down, and was destroyed by the light from above, conjured by Mr Rummage on the Island.

I knew the usurper. Why was I not afraid?

Rick and I entered the opening beneath the base of the wire. We were in a vast subterranean arena, a complex of spaces, above which rested the monumental disc.

Occasionally the whole clock-like province moved in powerful synchrony and the disc turned.

Across the arena were instruments and registers, and receptors, measuring, I guessed, pulses of light and energy, movements of heavenly bodies, and, I imagined, the co-ordinates of the passing sky vessels, even the distant heavens. There were no people.

Four passages led away from the area. Rick went over to look at one.

Beneath the wire, at the centre, where I stood, was the gaping hole that fell deep into the earth, from which I had seen the monstrous shape. It seemed like the tube of a telescope, or of a laser, or of a well. I moved forward to look down.

The dark hollow fell into an unimaginable abyss, which gave off a powerful energy.

I began to lose control. I felt like leaping forward. I saw myriad worlds in front of me, in a moment, far below the earth.

Deep in the morass of shadows, I saw another figure. This one wielded a huge hammer across an anvil of fire, casting a vast shape out of molten rock. It looked up.

What was using this darkness to look up to the stars? What did it seek? What was it doing?

I turned upwards to follow its gaze. There above me in the

191

dusk of heaven, I saw the shape that we had seen earlier at sea: a diagram, like a cross above a mountain range, linking certain peaks, amongst the stars.

What was this place? Who was controlling it? Where were the people? Suddenly, I felt weightless.

I began to panic. Had there not been soldiers outside, and figures threatening to enter? Where had Rick gone to? Would we find Jess? I called her name.

My legs gave way and all around me was rushing air. I was falling into the abyss. I felt it was the end.

But some power held my body. It pulled me up. My legs straightened and I steadied. I wiped my forehead and turned, breathless and shaking with fear.

The figure who had saved me looked at me.

She was wearing a white robe, and her long hair was partly hidden by a hood. She seemed to carry something in her left hand. Her eyes were composed, eyes of eternal under-standing, not only of this world. Eyes of eternal clarity, eternal purpose.

"Leave this place!"

She could see my frightened eyes. She pointed to a door.

I pointed to the wire column above us, which now obscured the sky. I remembered the night under the Dome with the figures arrayed around us, and the near incarnation of the Dark Master.

I began to fall again, but my hand was held.

I remembered the image from the painting in the Church of St Mary Magdalene. Somewhere in the background, almost out of sight, walked three figures in white robes.

The figure in front of me was one of them.

"I saw...."

"Leave this place! You do not have much time! What did you see?"

"A dark figure, like the Devil. The Dark Master. The one who wants to rule for eternity and lead us all down.

Who wants the Spearhead, who wants the knowledge, who wants...."

I stopped. My hand went involuntarily to the small of my back and felt for the object, the only thing I carried about me. The blood drained from my face. It was not there.

".... who wants to draw down the energy from the Universe, who wants to rule the Universe. We cannot escape. It is only a matter of time. Look, I nearly fell. Mr Rummage is wrong. We cannot win. We are lost!"

"I am here."

Tears ran down my face, from fear and helplessness and the loss of the object, which I could not admit to. My shame was complete. There was no relief. I fell to my knees and bent my head low.

"Who are you?"

"But you did not fall. And you also saw another figure. With an anvil. Remember, the dark is inhabited by more than one. There's a special providence...."

The figure chuckled.

"You have a time allotted to you. And a role. And an end. So does the Master of the Dark. His sins are eternal hubris and eternal hate. He is very powerful, because he preys on human weakness, the weakness that gives you the strength of choice. He too has a role, and a time. He is subject to the same laws, but he does not know it. He continues to try to destroy the light, by bribing, lying, bullying, surrounding himself with lesser energies, tempting false leaders with the riches of this world. But there is always a spark, something that will never die, will always hint at a better life. And finally, help destroy him.

There is always the dark, but you do not have to be consumed. That would be the end. And there will always be one to guide us out of it. One who forms images. But there is a terrible price. Now leave!"

"If you know the destiny of all of us, what is the purpose then?"

"And your good friends Jess, and Rick, who is somewhere behind us? He is a good boy, but he only sees so much. Look after him and Jess. There is sadness ahead, but do not fear. It will only be temporary. Have faith. One day your story will be told. When you have discovered the meaning of the object and how to make it grow. And recognise the true power of light and dark."

The figure held out her left hand. It contained the object that I call the cell.

I did not dare take it.

"You stole....!"

She looked at me.

She was about to hurl it into the abyss but I lunged forwards, nearly falling into the emptiness again.

I looked at her hand. It was empty. I felt again at the small of my back. The object was there.

"There must be a story in which people believe. There may be a prophet to live the story. There must be images to illustrate and draw down the power. Each of these can be corrupted and abused. But when the moment is right, as the cycle nearly reaches its nadir, and we are nearly there, the journey towards the light will begin again. There will be new hope. New symbols. And the cell will no longer only be in your keeping. The Infinite does not go away. We must find the Infinite, that some people call God. You remember that word you saw on the cross sword – "muchbuhijushin?""

I nodded.

"The mask of God changes, but the truth of the eternal energy remains the same. Always."

She chuckled again. Then her tone changed.

"As you were falling – just now – before I caught you. Did you see anything else?"

I thought for a moment. I recalled seeing the shape in the sky.

"You must find that place. However hard it is. Otherwise

194

the prophecy cannot be fulfilled. Do not be deceived. And remember this. You could only see it, as you were about to enter the abyss."

"But Mr Rummage told us to find the Island."

The figure became business-like.

"You must leave this place now."

I knew at once the two were connected. I touched her arm and felt its warmth. I moved to kiss her, but she held up her hand.

I heard Rick call me to come over and look. He was standing some distance from me. He seemed excited.

"I've found an exit," he said

The figure had pointed to it earlier.

I turned back to say goodbye. But the place was empty; the figure had gone.

I looked down into the gaping hole as I passed. Who was the blind figure I had seen wielding the hammer?

"Come on!" Rick called.

I caught up with him.

"I think I've found out what this place is. It's a kind of space monitoring station, connected to other sites. Over here," he moved towards a series of screens, "there are views of Doonwreath and other places. Most of the locations are coded it seems. I can't identify them."

I wondered if one of the sites might have been the Island.

It was clear that he had seen nothing of the lady.

He looked at me.

"Are you OK?"

"It's nothing. Come on! We must find Jess. We shouldn't have left her. Heaven knows what's been happening outside."

"We'll make for the beach as soon as we get out. The army will have those figures under control. You wait!"

"I hope she didn't try to follow."

We had forgotten that everything had stopped.

I led the way. Outside, one of the carriages was waiting and we leapt on. The door closed and the carriage moved forward at an amazing speed, reaching the outer wall in a few seconds.

The carriage was elevated upwards. A door opened and we ran out.

The evening sky was lit by what seemed an artificial light.

We were at the back of the building, which we had not seen before. There were several huts in the near distance, with two helicopters beside them.

Several military vehicles were stationed close the huts. To our utter horror, bodies lay strewn on the ground beside them.

A portly man in a suit was looking towards us. We dropped down in front of the carriage. He got into one of the vehicles, which moved away. Had he seen us?

A large boat was moored beside a landing stage behind the huts. From it, a row of figures was moving in our direction.

"Heavens!" I cried. "It's the boat we saw last night! That left the harbour at Dunemoor. The one that delivered the casket. The figures have come from the boat. They must know about....!"

Rick pointed.

Beyond the boat swirled the icy sea. Our only escape was out towards it, but there were other figures coming from that way too.

We made for a cutting, which led towards the helicopters, before turning seawards.

We followed this, keeping low and moving as fast as we could, pausing occasionally to peer over the top.

"Down!" I shouted. "The man's stopped and is looking this way!"

"I don't believe it!"

"It's Strangelblood!" We said together.

It was indeed, Mr Strangelblood, standing in his conceited glory, close to the wall, looking in our direction. Beside him was a figure, who I knew was the Stranger.

There were more soldiers' bodies on the shingle close to military vehicles, others on open ground, like the dead on an ancient battle field. Not one of the figures had been injured.

One man was tied, slumped, against a stationary carriage, his head bowed. It was Captain Blake. Alongside him was his mate, staring emptily out to sea.

"Are they alive?"

Neither of us was hopeful.

"What can we do?"

"Nothing. Hope to have a chance to avenge them. We'd better find Jess."

The figures were everywhere. Many were now on the building parapet. A few were guarding an entrance to the arena which was now open, others lined the base of the wall.

Still more were moving towards the open water, towards the point where Jess, we hoped, was hiding.

Our only chance was to make a run for it and get to the beach before the figures.

We went over the top, bent low and ran as fast as we could.

"Rick, Ty, where are you? Help...."

"Jess! Jess! We're coming now!" I screamed.

"They're...." Jess's voice faded.

We were running across the shingle, for the sea. Behind us, figures were moving at a steady pace, seeming to glide over the ground.

Rick moved right towards our camp. I kept on straight towards the beach.

Rick now ran at full speed. The figures sensed panic and increased theirs. They hurried towards the beach, Rick just ahead.

I swung back towards the camp.

The tent was still up, but there was no boat, and no Jess. The embers of the fire swirled upwards in the wind. The tide was very high.

Rick appeared from over the brow.

"Watch out! Rick!" I shouted.

The figures were nearly on him. Their invisible faces exuding hate.

I heard Jess's voice again and stopped dead in my tracks. She was barely audible.

A figure in the distance watched us.

Out to sea, the boat we had seen earlier, was waiting.

Its masts stood out against the glow of the night, sails unfurled.

Rick looked in the tent, took a burning stake from the edge of the fire, turned and hurried towards me.

I looked along the sea shore. I hoped that, somehow, Jess had made an escape. But there was no sign of her, or of our boat.

Other figures were heading towards the sea, some, way ahead; whilst a third group, to my surprise, were coming on to land.

Rick and I turned in desperation towards the open water.

As we did, I noticed something shiny on the beach. I picked it up and hurried on.

I am quite a good swimmer, but I would not have lasted long in the winter sea. The waves were choppy against the shoreline. I sensed a storm brewing.

We looked back. To our surprise, the figures who were chasing Rick had not turned, but continued straight into the sea, heading for some shallow craft some metres out.

I thought I caught Jess's voice on the wind.

We turned to see a canoe-like shape in the water, only a few meters out.

We waded out towards it.

Inside were a small inbuilt motor at one end, and a raised prow at the other. It could not have been more than three metres long. There was a set of controls in the middle of the boat, with symbols that I had not seen before.

Jess was lying at the bottom. Rompy, keeping guard, leapt up and tried to lick us.

"Jess! Jess! Rompy!" I cried, bending low. At first she didn't react, but then she opened her eyes.

Rick, up to his waist in water, held the side of the craft while I scrambled aboard. In the other hand, he held high the burning stake.

I helped Jess up, but I could see that she was in pain. There was blood on her temple. I wiped it clean and spoke to her softly. She smiled and tried to speak but I told her not to.

She wouldn't listen and proceeded to tell her story.

She had slipped and fallen badly having pushed our boat out to sea. She crawled along the shore until she saw the canoe-like craft. She heaved herself into it, to hide. The tide had risen and had carried her out. That is when she fell and lost consciousness.

She had with her a little food and water, though most stores were still in the sailing boat, which had drifted out to sea.

Rick, now up to his shoulders in water, pulled himself aboard.

Our situation was desperate. Rick and I could do little except paddle with our hands, and try to keep our heads down. Rick tied the ember to the prow, like a living thing.

We managed to get about fifty metres away from the beach.

Then we turned north and followed the shoreline.

Several figures guarded the beach, while others waded out to the mother ship. Captain Blake and his mate remained like gruesome trophies, close to Mr Strangelblood, now near the shore. He studied us carefully, as if biding his time.

Jess watched him through binoculars. The Stranger had gone.

"Why aren't they following us?" I asked.

"They're too busy taking over the world."

"I'd like to destroy them all. Except that they're not properly alive."

"I feel bad about Captain Blake, and his mate."

"What if they capture us?"

"Not if, when."

"We mustn't give up."

There was a pause.

"What exactly is this place? And why did Rumbags insist that we come here?"

"Did you see the craft overhead, Jess, and the energy pulses between it and the building?"

She nodded.

"Rumbags can't have known what might happen."

"I wish we had the Spearhead."

"We have the cell."

"A fat lot of good that is."

"We must overcome them. Somehow. Otherwise...."

There was a pause. I didn't mention the dark figure I had seen.

"I don't hold out much hope. I saw the.... devastation."

"Tell us, Jess."

"It was ferocious, very brief, and mostly one-sided. Captain Blake and his men fought hard. But they were overwhelmed by a force beyond them. Not a single enemy casualty and our soldiers and sailors wiped out. It was like the soldiers were dealing with dark matter itself. Poor devils.

We had no chance against them. Whatever power they have is unstoppable. We had no aerial back-up either."

"Perhaps the RAF couldn't fly over."

"What was happening inside the building?" asked Jess.

"We saw one figure; at least I did, but nothing else, though I could feel their presence. We watched the energy flows between the base and the sky-craft. Like power from heaven and hell. The station is linked to Doonwreath and elsewhere, Rick found out. We have to prevent them from falling into enemy hands."

"Before it is too late."

200

We had come to a standstill, as the wind was against us.

"What happened to the astrometer, Jess?" I asked.

To my amazement, Jess reached from under her coat and passed it to me.

"I had forgotten all about it. It became smaller," she said.

I looked at it and gave it back to her. It had a purpose, I was sure, that we didn't understand. I was pleased that she had it.

We began to move again.

"Did you notice, Ty," Rick said, "that the arena wires were made of the same metal that we found in the tunnel between Greenfields and Burnchester?"

"And were secured by climbing irons."

"We should report what's happened. Perhaps nobody else knows."

It was not much but it gave us hope.

"I'll send an SOS," said Rick.

He tried the handset, the main equipment being on shore, but there was no response.

All we could hear was the wind.

He tried again, in vain.

The whole country was in danger, that was obvious. Where would Mr Strangelblood attack next?

The cell, I was sure, must have a role, yet it seemed so trivial. It could do nothing, as far as I could see.

I had said nothing about the lady. I would mention it to Jess another time.

We began to move forwards slowly but made little progress. We were increasingly afraid of capture, and our mood worsened.

Then, without warning, there was a huge explosion from the Island.

Light impulses erupted from the ends of wires on top of the arena wall. Sparks and flames leapt into the sky.

Then everything went dead. Darkness covered the whole area where there had been brilliant light. It seemed as if the whole place had shut down, its energy expended. The humming ceased.

The wind intensified.

Our boat hit something.

"Heavens!" Jess shouted, pointing behind us.

Our prow had struck a small sailing boat – our very own.

Rick and I hurried to stop it drifting away, though the sway made it hard.

Rick managed to scramble aboard and hurl a line back to me. We transferred Rompy and our few possessions, then Jess and I got in.

In a few minutes we had the sails trimmed and set sail, with me at the tiller.

We gave a spontaneous cheer.

Our best hope was to out-sail the enemy ship, which Jess kept under observation, some way to starboard, against the full moon on the eastern horizon.

Several figures boarded the ship up a set of wooden steps against the bow.

These included what looked like prisoners. They tied Captain Blake's still slumped body to a mast alongside his mate.

Two enemy figures watched us carefully. Their stares struck my side even at this distance. I thought of Mr Blakemore and Mr Vespers. Different clothes. The same look.

A third prisoner, in the background, resembling Dr Bartok, was being led below.

I shouted at the top of my voice, helpless with fury. The others tried to calm me. We could do nothing for any of them, they said.

Slowly, we drew away from the enemy, and I calmed.

I thought of the hunched inchoate figure, with his dark anvil, in the abyss under the great inverted dome on Shingle Island. I looked through the transparent bottom of our boat into the deep of the sea. Nothing appeared and there were no recordings at all on the sonar screen. But I could sense an energy beneath us, troubled and wanting to break free, as if beginning to force the waves upwards into mountainous shapes, enhanced by the wind. An old sea deity was on the move. Something older than the god we thought we knew.

Dunemoor was not the only settlement beneath the eastern sea, and there were known submarine movements in these shallow waters. I looked and looked, thinking that there might be some way out beneath us, some other force perhaps, on our side, that could be called forth or which would appear in our desperate need.

The wind got up and I had difficulty holding the tiller, Rick and Jess struggled with the main sheets.

Gradually, we lost sight of the Island and left the enemy to starboard.

After about an hour, the wind dropped, and we managed to eat and drink a little. We were exhausted, but our determination grew.

# 14

We had to decide whether to anchor in one of the small coastal estuaries, before continuing; or whether to disembark and head inland.

Rick took the tiller, so that Jess and I could rest in the hold. The two of us began to sing. Our voices arose and fell, like the waves.

We took it in turns to sleep.

Rick's stake remained alight all this time, like an unyielding spirit.

Some time later I awoke and took over from Rick who needed rest.

The moon became shrouded and the wind increased.

Rick sat at the hold door, close to Jess, a shadow against the dark, the wind stretching the sail as I tacked north.

Rick had changed. He seemed to have grown. Perhaps it was me who had become more sensitive to these things, I do not know.

Rick tried the radio again.

He switched it on, and called into the mike.

"Mayday, Mayday, Mayday!"

His voice fell to nothing against the vast night waves.

There was no response, not even a crackling.

We waited quietly, hoping.

He tried other frequencies, called again. There was no

sound coming in, no message getting out. The system was dead. He threw it back into the hold.

He took a torch from one of the bags and tied it to the mast, as a sort of headlamp – not that it would have been seen from very far away, but it made him feel better. It was like a comrade for the still-burning ember. He looked at me and smiled.

"I'll take over if you like!" he said.

"I'm OK, thanks," I answered.

I could see him look out over the sea. Even at night there is a glow.

Then he wrapped a tarpaulin over his head so that he looked like a half-skinned fish.

Within minutes he was asleep.

Rompy looked up at me, then moved to the rim of the boat. He was agitated.

It must have been well after midnight when the storm started. I had felt strong gusts for some time, and stayed at the tiller watching the blackening sky, as long as I could.

Then the wind came at us like an eagle in a cage.

Rick and Jess woke.

The boat suddenly plunged down. Rick grabbed the side. Jess was thrown forward, and caught hold of one of the mainstays.

A massive wave nearly sank us, water pouring over the bow.

I screamed at Rick to drop the mainsail while I held the tiller. Jess started bailing out water.

I managed to get Rompy close to me.

Rick could barely hold on.

A second wave nearly threw him overboard, but he was saved by the boom which hit him hard. He fell clutching his head.

The free sail flapped wildly, then dropped into the sea, dragging us into a capsize. I thought we were finished.

I dropped the tiller and tried to pull the sail in. It was

trapped under the waves and wouldn't budge. If anything it was pulling us further down into the water.

Jess reached me and we began to haul it in. The boat re-balanced enough to keep us afloat, but the wind had swung us round aside the huge breakers, so that instead of facing the oncoming waves, we would be hit side-on.

We rose and fell, struggling for control. I got back to the tiller and tried to steer.

Rick had somehow crawled to the prow and released the jib. Jess was back bailing water, screaming as I had never heard her before. At the storm, at our fate, at God. There was a mixture of anger, fear and tears. We were easy prey.

We fought as best we could, but were thrown about, some-times being violently sick. This was a pitiless storm indeed.

Some of our things had come out of the packs and were blown overboard. We could do nothing. Letters, the docu-ments we saved, personal belongings, clothes, were hurled into the waves. The few clues to help us on, gone.

We stared helplessly as the astrometer, which had got loose, rolled overboard and sank beneath the swell.

The only thing to remain in position was the ember.

For a brief time the storm abated.

The sky cleared. What we had thought was the moon now passed over us. It was not the moon at all, but what seemed like, high in the atmosphere, a group of brilliantly lit planets or stars, in a particular formation, which, whilst on the horizon, had given us the impression of being whole. It had moved very quickly. It was in the shape we all knew, had already seen.

We cheered. Rompy started barking. We cheered some more. It must be a sign. A sign that we were on the right path. A symbol we could recognise. We cheered again. The sea was calmer now.

But it was not the stars which had disturbed Rompy, and he barked again. Behind us, at a close range, a ship rested on the waves; untouched it seemed by the terrible storm.

Like a hanging cloud.

The enemy ship. On which I had recognised Vipers and Blakemore, from another age.

We were wet and cold and near to collapse. We were desperate for food and water, and were now gripped with fear.

There was no escape. Nothing between us and certain capture and then....

Jess watched the ship, while trying to collect up what little was left of our belongings. Rick and I reset the jib and the mainsail. We had a chance, a small chance, of out-sailing her. It stood at some distance to starboard, watching us.

Soon we were sailing again. Jess managed to find us a scrap of bread, which we devoured, and some water. We began to make headway again, gradually distancing ourselves from the ship once more.

Rick told us a joke. We laughed loud and long, Rompy joining in the fun.

We decided to head for shore, which was not far to port.

We had to report what we had witnessed. Whatever power the enemy were using, seemed unearthly. Shingle Island was now in their hands.

Far more was at stake than we realised. We were being invaded, for sure, with no real idea who or what the enemy were.

Perhaps because of this, we began, truly, for the first time, to appreciate the necessity of our task. We were clear – even I was, despite my doubts – that the cell must be protected and taken to the Island off Scotland, as Mr Rummage had willed, and find its home. Before it was too late. There was just a chance.

The extraordinary sight of "our" constellation had given us hope. Was our destiny to take us beyond our known world?

Events at Burnchester seemed curiously present and real, as the enemy was now. But there was too much to do, to let future thoughts interfere with our present needs.

And the enemy was closing.

The enemy had orchestrated the powers of the dark, "drawing down power", the "hidden power of the universe", for its own purposes. And we knew what the consequences would be if we allowed them to win.

I told Rick and Jess that if we became separated, I would go on alone, to give the cell a chance of reaching its goal.

They said they would not allow it to happen, and would fight to the death to help and protect me.

As we made our way towards the shore, I wondered whether Mr Rummage had survived. Did he somehow know what had happened? The powers that he had previously invoked had not been revived. Perhaps he was, as Jess had said, dead. Perhaps they all were dead. We began to panic. We thought of our friends, John and David. Even of my enemy Julia. We realised how much we missed our old school, despite its horrors, and our friends.

Rick said that he would find Tom again for though nobody liked him – which we had falsely denied – he had been invaluable. It was true. We thought of our relatives, my mum and uncle, Jess's parents. Rick mentioned his uncle John. I thought of my father, who, from somewhere in this waste, was still guiding me. The cross-over between faith and belief, perhaps.

And now the first light of dawn arose. Just a shimmering light above the eastern sky. The vast expanse of empty sea re-emerged out of the night.

The great plane of water continued across to the horizon. I thought of the huge dark figure with the anvil that I had seen in the hollow beneath the arena. Who was this figure? What was it doing? It seemed to be preparing for something. It seemed to be searching for something. Was it blind?

I thought of our ancestors who worshipped the sun and the stars, and all the forces of nature. However much we had evolved, we had lost much in the process, that was clear.

The dawn gave us new hope, if only by its light. The sun began to dry us from the night's drenching.

We made good progress in the steady wind.

By mid-morning we could see sandy cliffs again, topped by trees.

A village seemed to lie beyond, capped by the church tower. How far it was from the cliff edge, we could not tell.

The place appeared very tranquil.

An empty shingle beach was now discernible. We were sailing well.

Jess was sitting, tiller in hand, recovered from her injuries.

Rick was standing beside her, looking landward. We aimed to hide the boat and return to it later, for our journey northward.

We took our depleted packs, ready for landing.

We would have to tack on our approach to the beach.

We hadn't noticed the storm cloud behind us to the east nor the ship closing upon us.

We approached the point where the two opposing gusts collided, forming a tumultuous upsurge of water. We strapped our packs on. I took Rompy's lead and tied it around me.

We instinctively came together and hugged each other.

We didn't speak, yet we were closer than ever before.

Rick was letting down the mainsail, just as the wave hit. Jess stopped him from going overboard, though both fell hard.

I leapt to take the tiller and tried to turn the boat into the wind. It was our only chance. In doing so, the wind hit us harder. I lost control, and the boat lurched to port.

Out of the corner of my eye, I noticed three figures, as if riding on the waves, like shadows, approaching our boat.

Rick grabbed the lit stake, and held it aloft, as the boat heaved.

Another wave hit us. Rick and Jess were thrust overboard into the heaving water.

I was thrown sideways but managed to cling to the mast. I could just make out Jess and Rick in the waves. I wanted to go to them, but it was useless.

I screamed out as loud as I could, at the unknown forces that were hurled against us. At the injustice and the sadness of it. Rompy, dear thing, started to bark, and then leapt at the mast as if it was an enemy. As ever, telling me something.

Jess looked at me from the sea. She was trying in her desperate struggle to tell me something. They were eyes of love.

The three figures were closing in on them both.

They threw ropes over them. It was clear that they were waiting for me to follow.

I grabbed one of the sheets that held the mast, and tried to break it loose, but it would not budge.

Rick and Jess were struggling with the ropes around them. I went to help, but Rick shook his head, pointing with the burning stake that he still held. Jess screamed for me to swim.

The ember set alight the side of the boat which held the sheet in place. Rick then turned it on the ropes about them, as they were being dragged towards the enemy ship.

The fire intensified, and the sheet flew into the air like a spring. The mast cracked under the strain, and fell. I wrapped one arm about it with Rompy under the other, and pushed it over the side of the boat into the sea.

The figures were on the far side of the burning vessel, which gave off an intense heat, and erupted into flame. Nothing could get close to it, nothing come round to get me.

I lifted Rompy onto the thickest part of the mast. The crossbar allowed us to float like a raft.

I tried to manoeuvre, but the wind and tide were too strong. I tried to swing onto the mast, but I was too big, and slid backwards into the sea. I clung on desperately, sensing the cold creep along my legs and into my body.

I vowed to repay the love that I had been shown, if ever I could.

I prayed – yes, again – that Rick and Jess would somehow overcome the figures. Perhaps the torch would save them too.

I could see little but the swell and the waves, and only wisps of smoke rising some distance off. The wind and water troubled my eyes.

Then the dark ship appeared at the edge of the storm cloud. I saw figures climbing the steps, followed by two prisoners, a living ember held high. The ember gave me hope, and I gave a muted cheer.

The tide drove me shoreward. I would never give up hope of seeing my friends again.

"The waters move forever along the shore
Rolling in strangest harmony on the low stones."

I lost consciousness.

*

As we moved through the water, a dark figure emerged from the bottom of the sea beneath me.

It seemed to control the waters and be giving commands to the enemy boat. It seemed to look in the direction of my shadow above, but remained still, undecided.

Further out to sea, another figure rose from the waves, and stood over me, sheltering me from the shadow below. The forces arraigned on either side of me, were ready to do battle for my life.

*

As I drifted I dreamed that I awoke to the sound of a dog barking. Rompy was holding my collar, and had saved me. I stretched up and gave him a hug. His tail wagged, but he was weak.

I needed to get ashore and find drink and food.

*

I am taken down into the depths and see the ancient city.

I manage to escape by fleeing along the tunnels under the sea, only to come up again in the strangest place I have ever seen.

*

Then clouds darken and I am struggling to reach the shore after the violent storm, onto a shingle beach. Jess and Rick have gone. The boat has gone. My little smiling dog has gone. I hold only a few things. As I crawl ashore amidst the shrinking waves, I see a momentous figure straddling them, beckoning to take me down.

I know I am close to where we saw the lights. I am sorry if I seem confused but I can only repeat the images as they come.

For a moment I stand back from my tears – the music can't deceive me for long – and imagine my memories thrown onto one of Dr Bartok's screens. What language would he find? What pointers to that future that he and others so strenuously seek and try not to fear? How would these images be revealed, and then interpreted?

*

The lights had emerged; at least that is what Rick had said, from close to the shore, or from the forest nearby. They seemed to arise and drift into the air, and hold there for several seconds and then move at an amazing speed. We had all heard of the great Suffolk mystery and we had been warned by Mr Greenshank not to be afraid. But seeing them, exposed in the night sea, caught us unawares, and when they passed, left us paralysed in an inability to speak.

We saw the lights twice. Though it was night, there was a moon beyond the storm clouds far inland. They were not anything we had seen before. Rick wanted to follow them, find out where they had come from, what they were, but we were at sea, and had no chance.

We knew that they were important, but did not, could not know why.

I remember then thinking they were UFOs, but Jess laughed and said that they were simply military aircraft, reminding us that Mr Greenshank had told us to look out for them, though her voice belied her certainty.

*

My dream, which I know I will write down sometime, if I can remember it, is a series of images, containing truth.

*

First storm:
The faces of my friends, Jess and Rick, somehow disparate, from another time, and yet familiar, are calling to me. I feel older, watching myself asleep. The boat at sea. Three young people helplessly lost on the northern swell, cold frightened, mocked. Neptune wheels his Trident. He wants recognition, a sacrifice.

The food is gone; the parcels have been washed overboard, containing our instructions, giving us clues to the way. We hug each other to keep warm, murmur songs to keep us in good spirits, helplessly struggling to stay alive.

The sea calms, the sun bursts forth, we dry, and drink the remainder of the water, a painful smile upon our faces. The wind and swell have taken us north it seems, but we do not know.

A plume of cloud draws a line across the sky, like a passing plane. It seems to come from somewhere inland. We think we know, but dare not say.

*

Second storm:

After the first storm, there came another. So sudden, so ferocious that we hardly had time to speak. We struggled to face the wind and waves. We knew our time had come, our separation imminent. Yet in that moment, or moments rather, we felt closer than we had before. The sadness could not over-come the closeness, the past and present stronger than the future, now.

When the wave hit, I remember one thing that Jess said.

"It is Burnchester that has burnt. That was the smoke that stretched across the sky." Even fighting for her life she wanted to tell me this and then she told me that we would meet again.

It was as if the sea was exacting retribution for the flames. The tide that had crept up the beach, snugged along the river banks, across the flatlands, lifted the rotting timbers en-meshed in the weedy sides. Perhaps it was the swollen river that smothered the flames.

A mass of water hit the bow and threw our boat into the air. She turned in the wind. The spray and wind were one. I caught a glimpse through the glassy sea of Jess and Rick hold-ing hands in a gesture of defiance, smiling, almost, as they hit the water; then I myself was taken down.

*

The City Beneath the Sea. Suddenly, out of the storm, but still in the turbulent waters, it was there, in its murky glory.

Straddling the old river mouth, across the sea bed which I now surveyed. A harbour with many ships. Churches, a castle, a market, people weaving in and out. Bells, cries. Horses and their loads along the busy roads. Priests in robes of black.

I came up for air, almost against my will, bewildered by what I had seen. The furious storm above; the living city below. I drew in as quickly as I could. I swallowed sea water. I fought for air, trying to lift my head above the swell.

The boat was nowhere to be seen. There was no Jess, no Rick, the sea threw me up and sucked me down in a troubled cycle, like a baby in a cradle. The rain streamed down with the wind and spray. I could not fight it, but like a drowning insect beat slowly, trying to save energy, weakening by the minute, tempted by what I had seen, afraid I would never return.

I tried to look across the water. There was nothing. Just a trident above the waves.

I tried to swim away, in vain. I took in more water and spewed it out, choking as the current drew me down. I cannot go on. What have I seen? I want to go back. But I do not want to die. I try to scream, but the water takes me again, throws me over, a plaything of the Gods.

Everything is lost. I am alone. Apart from the wooden mast to which I cling. As if by chance, it came. Crucified upon the waves.

I struggle to tie myself to it, but the water jealously breaks my grip. My frozen hands can hardly move. I am driven back. I frantically clasp a line of rope and with all my remaining strength try to haul myself to the mast.

*

The helicopter crew had done their best, but it was too dangerous to continue. They will search again, no doubt, when it is light. They have not seen me. But they have something else to report.

What were those lights in the sky? The secret research stations are known to them. The flights of experimental craft, above top secret, that emerge into the night from the banks of the subtle shore, out of nowhere it seems, from the wind-swept reeds, from the shiny caverns below, from which time and science dance. They may not know the detail, but they know that they are there. And these were different.

# 15

FRANCE

High on a mountain in South West France a man and a woman look out onto the surrounding landscape. They have been waiting in this wilderness for days.

The colours of ragged flowers and the scents of late herbs, hang suspended in the winter sun.

The ground shows a patchwork of light and shade, which feels like the waves of a mountain sea, as the clouds hurry over the sun.

The man scans the upland rock and hidden gorges.

A shimmer comes off the mountainside, the beginnings of an evening mist.

He focuses on a clump of birch scrub, crossed by what might be a pathway, possibly an animal track. He closes in on a shape.

"It could be someone. Or something. I'm not sure," the man says.

The woman watches the valley path below.

There is rough parking area close to the foot of the opposite hill, from which a stony track leads upwards.

"How can you be so sure they will come?" she asks.

"They have to come."

The man rests his binoculars on the stump of a juniper.

The shape appears to have gone. Or has it changed with the light?

The landscape is full of shadows, the spirits of the one-time residents, present still.

Perhaps they are waiting to be recalled to life – so that they might finish their time on earth, as had been written. Before Holy Church broke their pact with Fate, bled them like sickled barley. Fate always takes revenge.

This is Cathar country, early keepers of the tradition, protectors of the secret. The Knights Templar are their heirs. The Priory claim a direct line.

The ruined walls of Montsegur cling to a summit over the valley, where the Cathars were trapped, then burned. Except for the few who escaped carrying the secret that could destroy the Church. Hidden, guarded for centuries. Taken by sea to a refuge, the site of the ancient stones.

Where the parchment has been found.

Cries of the burning can be heard on the wind. The woman, a painter, absorbs the sepulchral light of early dusk. Snow lies only on the highest peaks.

The landscape itself seems to be watching.

"My source in the Holy See has never let me down. They will want to be here first. Do you remember our visit last summer?"

A cry above them. An eagle makes its way along the upper valley.

"The Valley of the King. Sounds almost Egyptian. The burial place of some ancient ruler, did we not think?"

"Of their King, we assumed, although I'm beginning to think it might be something else. Something even more important."

"What?"

"A link to the Spearhead."

The woman thinks of the last class she took before the attack at Burnchester.

Tears form in her eyes. They were lucky to escape. What of their colleagues, the parents, the children?

She imagines the children marching up the valley towards the castle, singing.

An animal runs, twisting between the rocks of the upper valley.

It is too late.

The eagle has closed its wings.

There is the drawn-out cry of death.

The bird rises into the air, carrying its prey, towards the broken castle wall.

"There! Down there, by the car park!"

They lower their heads.

"Keep absolutely still."

Four people move along the path.

"Hikers?"

"I don't think so."

They have engaged forces older and greater than themselves. An enemy able to murder a Bishop, behind which lies a dark force of irredeemable power, bent on ruling the world.

It is not just the Church of Rome that wants to examine the site, as they have the document found by Tyro and her friends, but all others who, involved in the pursuit of power, secular or religious, have an interest too, for good or ill.

Given the history of repression against those who seek a broader truth, the dangers are immeasurable.

A car appears on the road from the north, and parks.

"Reinforcements, if I am not mistaken. We must be careful."

"The Church has long suspected the existence of the ancient tomb. The parchment confirmed our discovery. The Priory must have passed it to them. Having murdered the Bishop to get it."

"What will they do when they reach the site?"

"Perhaps destroy it."

"If the Church and the Priory find it is what they think, they can do another deal."

"If it is something more, as I now think, even they might turn back."

"And Mr Strangelblood?"

"Mr Strangelblood, remember, is not the Priory. His aim is universal domination.

The Priory saw that Tyro was given something important. If they can get what Tyro possesses, Mr Strangelblood can be managed. The Church does not know what Tyro holds."

"Which is why the Priory are after her and what she has. It is the final piece in the jigsaw, that will give them absolute control."

"Like a new story, a new myth to usurp the old?"

"Perhaps it will then be the Church's turn to make a deal?"

"Perhaps, though the Church and the Priory are closer than we think."

"You mean they are one and the same. How can that be?"

"Not quite one and the same. But tied to each other's destiny. One pre-dates the other. Now it is time for the other which was usurped, to return."

"Like the return of a King?"

"Like the return of an older wisdom, though in a new form. The secret of which lies partly in Tyro's hands, but also, if my understanding is right, partly here at the site we are going to. For I suspect that whilst it may indeed be the burial place of a King, it is also something older, which neither the Church nor the Priory know of, for their eyes are blinkered by their own pride, and their ignorance of time and destiny. Those forces are on the move, with the greatest creator of them all, who perhaps can be found somewhere here too."

"Who?"

The first group of walkers are joined by the three from the vehicle. These are cloaked.

"Let's go. We still have a long way to go. We can cut to the other side of the valley which will lead to the Valley of the King. I want us to be there before them. We have three days march."

The man crawls forward along the rough ground, dragging his rucsac. The woman follows.

"If that *was* someone on the hill above we must be doubly careful," she says.

They move forward through the rough landscape as it gets darker.

Since their momentous discoveries in the area the previous summer – the film that turned the Bishop of Dunemoor pale – and of the document at Burnchester, and of their return here, the rules of the game have changed.

History has become a living war, for the truth and the ultimate energy. Their currency, the management of deception. Mr Rummage knew that, but he has disappeared, perhaps by his own intentions.

After about an hour, they drop down into a gully.

They drink out of a stream. A magnificent view lies below them. A beautiful valley leads upwards into the high mountains.

"There is another reason to be here. The Priory and the Church of Rome are not the only seekers of this information. There are other institutions and agencies across the globe who would want it too. Power always has a price. The highest source of power has the highest price. And the market is global.

It is their task to make sure that the knowledge does not fall into other enemies' hands. And to prevent them from getting too close to the Valley or the Tomb that we filmed last year. The tomb that the Priory and the Church must visit, before anyone else can spoil the ground.

For the ultimate secret that will change the destiny of the developed world. The secret for which Rome would not hesitate to seek the ultimate price. With which their future to Eternity would be secure."

Across the valley the castle ruins show a precipice on one side, and steep declines on the other three. On one of these a track can be made out, like a scar.

"It is so beautiful," Miss Peverell says. "I wouldn't have believed that it is a place of pain."

"I was right," the man says.

The woman lifts her binoculars.

"The fifth in the group. The first wearing a cloak. Of those who came by car. It is a figure that I recognise."

"Recognise? Who?"

"The one they call the Stranger."

# 16

I run onto the platform, pushing my way through the crowds, waiting for the early trains. The clock shows one minute before midnight. If I miss my train I am doomed. There are police everywhere.

"This is an emergency passenger announcement. Repeat: an emergency passenger announcement. Will.... a, Ms Tyro Wander.... repeat Ms Tyro Wander, believed to be travelling on the.... report to the Station Master's office."

A headline reads: "Missing girl escapes. Wanted."

The news slams against my brain amidst the tannoy's arrivals and departures. I scan the noticeboard for my platform. Train times are flickered up.

The gate ahead is closed. It is my train. It has started to move. The board beside it announces: "The Flying Highlander".

I double my effort but the guards block my path. I run to their left, swing round a tall column and jump the barrier, as the train gathers speed.

I run alongside an empty train.

I leap on, scramble to a far door, drop down, run across the track and up onto the empty platform, as my train moves steadily on.

I race forwards, my heart pumping, kicking in, and just reach the last door. To my amazement, it opens. A hand stretches out and pulls me aboard.

I fall to the floor, the door slamming behind me. But the person who helped me has gone.

Security guards hurry down the platform. A call is put through to stop the train.

I stagger to the next compartment and look out of the open window. I nearly choke. Three figures have broken through the barrier.

The throb of the engines gives a heavy beat. The train increases speed.

"Please, God," I whisper.

The guards try to stop the figures, but they are brushed aside.

The figures glide towards the last carriage, whose door, to my horror, is being held open by a bony hand.

The train approaches the end of the platform. The figures move faster. The guards cannot catch up, and raise their rifles. Why has the train not stopped? Something is wrong.

"Halt or we will fire!"

The leading figure stretches out a hand in a desperate effort to reach the last door. The train rumbles on.

"Halt or we will fire!"

The leading figure lunges again. The other two cannot make it. The voice calls again. The first figure just catches the hand, as the last carriage heads for the open track.

The two remaining figures cover the first. There are shots. The leading figure is pulled aboard, and the door swings shut.

The other two veer into the dark waste ground beside the track, blood streaming from their backs.

The train gains speed. There is a whistle. We have left the platform.

I look out again, shaking. The guards have followed the wounded figures, and police are everywhere.

Somewhere on board is the other figure. Instead of escaping into safety, I am more trapped.

I hurry along the corridor, trying to steady myself. The

sight of the hand brings back the horror of the Burnchester figures, and of those in the shadows at Downing Street. Their presence makes me angry, but my determination increases. I am sworn to do what I can. Who is there left but ourselves?

At least the cell is with me and I carry my aunt's medallion. That is all I have. No map, no money, no friends. All I know is that I am heading north. For Doonwreath and the Island. Will I be too late? I am not hopeful. Everyone is after me.

The first few carriages are sleepers and most compartment doors are shut.

I pass some travellers. I reach the restaurant car. I squeeze past the bulky waiter who is setting out places.

Towards the far door, a ticket collector asks for my ticket. I have left it in my compartment, I say, apologising. He looks down at me. Which one? Number seven, coach C, I answer, looking into his face. He looks at me and says he will come back later. After all, there is not much chance of escape. I am cautious.

The ticket collector passes the waiter and is distracted by someone ahead, calling.

I move on. The automatic doors close. This carriage is dimly lit and quiet.

City lights flash past the windows, as does a station. There are police on the platform. The train slows. My heart beats fast. I expect it to stop, but it runs on.

My only chance is to find an empty compartment. I try each door. The first is locked. And the second, and the third. I continue, in vain.

Will the figure follow me now, or later? Is there more than one? Who pulled me up? Was it the same hand? They cannot know that I know that they are on board. A slight advantage. They can afford, perhaps, so they think, to take their time.

Two passengers are coming my way. I turn towards the window. I have a strange feeling as they pass, but neither stops. I think I recognise one of them. My heart misses several beats.

I stumble on.

There is a tunnel ahead.

Through the window, I can see the first three carriages. One more sleeper, then lights and tables, and fellow travellers sitting. It will be a long night for them. Perhaps this is my chance. In the open. I need rest. It seems friendly. My hopes rise.

I hasten through the last sleeper, trying each door. The corridor seems darker than the others. My hopes fade as I reach the dividing door to the open carriages.

It is locked. I try it again, but it will not budge. I wave through the door window to a passenger on the other side. I beat the window with my fist. The man looks up.

"Open the door!" I call, trying not to speak too loudly.

The man carries on reading.

I beat the window furiously. The man doesn't respond. I stare at him. I smile. I point to the door handle. He doesn't even notice me.

I turn back angrily. My one chance has gone. I have nowhere to go.

The train races through the night.

The lights of the city flicker by. Perhaps I can break a window? Or escape at the next station? And where will that be? Two hundred miles to the north? And the figures close at hand!

The North. I look out of the window, trying to think, but I cannot. I broke free of the Stranger and Mr Strangelblood but here I am trapped. The snow is falling heavily now. How much longer do I have? The ticket collector will find me soon. I am easy prey.

The battle is just beginning. The candle is still alight, but flickering. I think of Rick and Jess. I will not give in.

I do not know what keeps me going. Perhaps it was a voice.

I certainly heard a voice, as if out of the rumbling of the train over the compounding snow. Was it the voice of my father, or of my mother? Perhaps it was Jess or Rick, even Tom, or, I hoped, against hope, that of Jules. I did not know, for it was unrecognisable, as if its point of origin had been in the universe above, calling from a far, far distant place. Calling me through the night sky.

I did not care who it was, though looking back now, I missed Jules most. My mum was kind of with me anyway. And my Dad too.

I try each door, again, in vain.

Someone is coming. My heart beats faster. I clutch the cell. I think of another disguise, but how can I? Except by manner, or inner mask?

I adjust my aunt's medallion as the figure approaches. There is a pause. A horrible energy. The figure sees the pendant. It is about to speak, when someone taps its shoulder. It is the conductor.

The conductor asks the figure if he might see his ticket, please.

A moment's confusion. The figure turns angrily, and they move back to the light. I stare in horror. It is the Stranger.

I want to be sick. There is an argument.

If only I could disappear. I am on the edge of the abyss.

There is a crashing of the door from the open compartment.

A man, back bowed and hand badly hurt, runs past me.

I try another door. The argument behind me is intensifying. There are still a few doors to try.

The voices lower. The argument is settled, or is it something worse? The next door, I think. I clutch the cell, and pray. If only I could hide. I take the object from my pocket.

In my hand is a key. I stare in amazement. I place it in the lock and turn the handle.

The door opens. I can't believe it! Gasping, I enter. I close the door behind me and lock it, as tightly as I can.

I let my small bag fall to the ground. The light is dim, but it is enough for me to make out a figure sitting near the window. Flakes of snow brush the pane.

There is a knock behind me. I scream. The sitting figure continues to look forward.

Someone calls my name from the other side of the door. It is a voice that I know. I open it, hesitating, in case it is a trap. The person falls into the compartment. The door slams behind him. He turns and our eyes meet.

"Jules!" I cry, my heart pounding.

We throw our arms around each other.

"I told you I was not going to let you go alone!"

I step back.

"I think all is lost. The Stranger is on board. He tried to talk to me. I do not know what to do. If only...."

There is a light cough behind me.

I turn.

In front of me, still sitting, but with his face now to the window, is the incomplete image of a man. I can see his reflection looking out into the night. There is a moment's silence before he turns towards me. Our eyes meet. I recognise him at once, though he seems older.

Tears swell up in my eyes. I edge towards him, disbelieving.

Jules remains motionless.

The image smiles, shyly, at first. Guilty, even, as if he were an intruder. But the look on my face, and then my touch on his shoulder, reassures him. I move towards him, as he tries to get up, but he seems too weak. We hold out our hands, and I bend to hug him.

"Dad?" I whisper through my tears. "Can it really be you?"

He wraps his solid arms around me. I think I sense the good spirits who appeared beneath the Abbey Church, close by us, as if keeping guard.

"You're looking good. I knew you'd make it. You've

become the hero of your own story at last! I never lost faith. Never give up hope. I'll see you again. Say hello to Mum! Love you. Always. Always."

I try to hold the figure but it is dissolving. He struggles to remain but his eyes, now full of tears, begin to fade, though I see them still.

I try to speak, but no words emerge. Tears wash away my gentle father's half-arisen face, and he disappears from where he came.

I feel Jules' hand on my shoulder, and turn. I do not ask if he saw my father too, though I believe he has. He respects, that is all; something beyond our knowledge or understanding. I am glad that he is here. I never lost faith, and nor has he.

We look into each other's eyes. We both want to speak. We both start to but can't continue. We are too happy.

Jules carries my old cross-sword, the one that he recovered from the figure. He hands it to me.

"Remember."

"Of course. But it is yours now. I do not care about objects anymore. I have my friend back."

I take his hand and draw him closer to me and hug him and kiss his cheeks. We hold each other tightly.

I break off. I draw back and look serious.

"Can we make it?" I whisper.

"We have to."

"I guess so."

"We have no choice. We must go forward as best we can. We will make it! Together! We have to reach Doonwreath, before the enemy."

"And you will find your father," I say.

Tears begin to form in my eyes. It still matters. It was my pact, to myself, and to my lost parents, who I know guide me still.

The train hurries through the night, heading north. The

North of Tyro's dreams, where there will be mountains and snow.

It is snowing heavily outside.

Jules takes something out of his bag.

"I got us some tickets."

I hug him again. "Brilliant! How long is the journey?"

"A day, perhaps more. The snow has been falling for several days in the North. Behind us, there is trouble everywhere."

"Everyone is after us."

I say nothing of the Stranger or of the figures.

It is for this that I have been preparing. It is for this that now I know I am ready.

For the journey into the unknown. To find the Island. And a home for the cell.

Other books in the Burnchester mystery

The Mysterious Burnchester Hall
The Burnchester Dome and the Sacred Cell